LOST
GENERATIONS

Steven Noble

LOST
GENERATIONS

Steven Noble

Lost Generations is a work of fiction.

Names, characters, places and incidents are the products of the author's imagination
or are used fictitiously. Any resemblance to actual events, locales, or persons, living
or dead, is entirely coincidental.

Cover design by Rita Petithory

Book design by Rita Petithory

Printed in the United States of America

The Troy Book Makers • Troy, New York • thetroybookmakers.com

To order additional copies of this title, contact your favorite local bookstore
or to purchase this book online visit www.tbmbooks.com or www.amazon.com

ISBN: 978-1-614681-502

To my wife, Donna and children,
Keith, Christopher and Katherine.

I love you all dearly.

PROLOGUE

JOE NUNEZ WAS ON the second floor of the house when he heard the commotion bubbling up from below. Hank, his second-in-command, came puffing up the stairwell. "Boss," said Hank, "you gotta get down to the basement!"

"We don't need this right now," said Joe. "We're already two days behind on this job and we don't need any more delays. This better be good and we better be able to solve it quickly. What's going on, Hank?"

"Not exactly sure what's going on! I heard a loud gasp from Manny in the basement and then he and the two other workers came running up the stairs. They were crossing themselves and chattering in Portuguese so fast I couldn't understand a word they were saying. When they speak slowly, I get the gist of what they're saying, but all I got out of this commotion was "bebe" and "morte" and that made no sense at all. I think you're going to need to translate."

Joe sighed. Manny was one of his best workers, normally unflappable. He walked downstairs and saw the three workers in the foyer of the house. He stopped as he saw them get ready to light cigarettes. "Whoa, what the hell you guys think you're doing? We have paint thinner and scraps of wallpaper all over the floor! You're going to start the whole place on fire. What the hell is going on here?"

The three of them looked at him in disbelief. They all started yelling at him at once. "Stop," said Joe. "One at a time, real slow, in English. Manny, you first."

Joe could see Manny at a loss for words. "Boss," said Manny, "we found the baby in the basement." The words came slowly. Joe could tell that Manny was thinking in Portuguese and slowly translating the words into English.

"What do you mean you found the baby in the basement, Manny? The house was locked overnight while we were gone. How could anyone have put a baby down there?"

"I found it in the coal chute, boss," said Manny. "It's dead!"

"What do you mean its dead? How do you know that? Somebody Dial 911 and call for EMTs!"

"No boss! It's really dead. I think it's been there for a long time." Manny wasn't hesitating anymore; he knew exactly what he was saying.

Joe looked at the other two workers. They were both nodding their heads in agreement with Manny. Shit, thought Joe, this is going to be bad. "You guys didn't touch anything did you?" asked Joe. He looked at the three of them. Two of them were shaking their heads no and one was nodding his head yes. "Okay, show me what's down there." Now they all shook their heads no. Clearly, none of them were going to go back down to the basement. "Hank, tell everybody to stop what they're doing and get out of the house. No running, no panicking, and leave everything in place, but nobody leaves the yard. Call 911 and tell them to send the police here! Then come downstairs into the basement because if these guys are wrong, I may have to send you back upstairs to call for EMTs."

Joe went down the stairs to the basement. It was quiet down there. Work lights were on and it was bright. There were tools all over the place, abandoned by the workers as they ran up the stairs. He walked past a partially dismantled furnace to the far wall where the coal chute was. The door was gaping wide open and he could see what looked like some old yellowed newspapers and what look like a baby blanket. He turned on his flashlight and gasped. The blanket had been partially opened and he could see the dried-up face of a baby, sunken eyes, curled up lip, no teeth. He crossed himself and started to say a prayer. He heard Hank coming down the stairs but he held up his hand and backed away from the chute. He could faintly hear sirens in the distance.

Chapter 1

JACK DEL RIO sat on the fantail of his boat in Snug Harbor, Rhode Island, surprised by the phone call that he had been waiting for for the last twenty years.

"This is Detective Phil Hudson of the Newport police; I am looking for Dr. Jack Del Rio."

"This is Dr. Del Rio."

"Good afternoon Dr. Del Rio," said Phil. "We would like to discuss a phone call you made to the Newport police 20 years ago regarding a possible missing baby. You could come by the station or my partner and I could meet you somewhere. "

"I see," said Jack, his pulse racing slightly. "I will be working in Providence tomorrow and I can probably stop by the station late in the afternoon."

"That would be fine," said Phil. "I will be expecting you and when you get to the station, just tell the desk sergeant that you want to speak to me."

Jack sat quietly for a few more moments; nursing his drink and feeling the boat float up and down on the small chop in the Salt Pond. He felt the wind through his receding hairline. Only wind could produce a chop this deep into the protection of the break water, up from the narrow inlet between Galilee and

Jerusalem. He loved the peace and quiet that sitting on the boat afforded him as he watched the sunset. He expected that this was going to be the last quiet he would have for the next several weeks while all this was sorted out.

His mind wandered back to that day twenty years ago, one that had produced the most difficult decision of his career and had led unfailingly to this phone call. Jack had been sitting in the call room when the original call came from the delivery room about a potential transport to his service. These calls were almost always about a patient in some distress in labor and Jack was surprised to hear that the call was about a non-pregnant patient. He remembered the paint peeling on the wall, the scratched remote he used to mute the wall mounted TV and the creaky bedsprings as he sat up to answer the transferred phone call.

"Hi Jack," said Bob Carter, "I was glad to hear it was you on call tonight. I have a patient I'd like to transfer to you that I think you can help me with. She is a 20 year-old, gravida zero, coed at Salve Regina College who came into the emergency room with heavy vaginal bleeding. Her uterus is 8-9 times normal size and an ultrasound in our emergency room suggests that she has a large fibroid."

Jack remembered listening to the desperation in Bob's voice and being surprised by it. He knew Bob very well. Bob had graduated from the residency program several years ahead of Jack. Bob had always been very good at deflecting extra work to others but had always been supremely confident in his capabilities. This girl must be in real trouble. Jack decided to accept her immediately. He almost always accepted patients like this with the feeling that they were better off in his care than in the care of someone who was frightened and worried about their outcome.

"Sure, you can transfer her up to us. Tell me a little bit more about her condition," said Jack.

"She is quite anemic and her vital signs are starting to deteriorate; she has a rapid pulse of 135 and a marginal blood pressure of 90/60. She is also febrile with a temperature of 102.8 F. I've already given her two units of blood!" Jack's again noted that his colleague sounded desperate.

"Send her to our accident room along with her latest labs and blood type and I'll call our accident room and tell them that she's coming. What's her name?" Jack remembered being uncomfortable because he knew that there was virtually no truth to the cover story that was supposedly prompting this transfer. Young girls virtually never grew large fibroids that caused sudden life-threatening bleeding. Something else was going on and it was likely to be bad. Uterine cancer and molar pregnancy immediately came to mind.

Jack called the accident room and told them to expect this patient's transfer from Newport Hospital. Jack then called his covering chief resident, Kathryn O'Connell. "Kate, we have a young lady being transferred to us from Newport Hospital who's having heavy vaginal bleeding. Get the ultrasound room ready so we can scan her and also bring a flashlight and a speculum so we can do a vaginal exam on her."

"Sure, Dr. Del Rio," said Kate, "I'll get the room ready but I'm a little confused at why we would need a speculum and flashlight in the ultrasound room."

"You'll see," said Jack. He loved it when he mystified residents, especially chief residents. He would show Kate another new trick tonight that would help her next year when she would be the attending doctor.

The patient, Mary Murphy, looked very anxious as they

wheeled her into the ultrasound room. She was thin, with dark hair and a very pale complexion. Jack sat on the edge of the stretcher and held her hand. "Hi, I am Dr. Del Rio and this is my chief resident Kate. It sounds like you have been bleeding pretty heavily and you look frightened. Why don't you tell us how all this started?"

"I started bleeding three days ago," said Mary. "At first I just thought it was a regular period but then the bleeding kept getting heavier and heavier. This afternoon I felt a little lightheaded and almost fainted so I decided it was time to go to the accident room."

"Have you ever had anything like this before?" asked Jack.

"No, never."

"Have you had any problems with bruising or excess bleeding with cuts?" asked Jack.

"No, never."

"Have you ever been pregnant or could you be pregnant now?" asked Jack.

"No, never."

Jack chatted with her for a few more minutes and got a lot of "no, never" answers on topics like contraception and sexual activity. She did reveal that her last and only visit to a gynecologist had been two years ago, just before she started college, and she had no problems at that time. He asked her if she'd ever been told she had a fibroid but she answered that she did not know what a fibroid was. While he was speaking to her, he performed an abdominal ultrasound which showed the top of her uterus reached her umbilicus. There were bright white echoes inside the uterus which suggested to him that she had a retained placenta! No part of this scan was consistent with a fibroid uterus. Kate's eyes had grown wider as she watched this information unfold on the screen as Jack continued his quiet conversation with Mary.

Chapter 2

DETECTIVE ANTONIO FUENTES had come together with his team. Tony was a career policeman, thin and acerbic looking with the yellowed fingers of a lifelong smoker. He had been a lead detective for 15 years. He sat with Philip Hudson, his partner for the last 8 years. Phil was a little chunky, with rumpled clothes but a perfectly organized sheaf of notes, labeled "Baby Doe, Thames Street." The third member of the team was Sheila Goldstein with a freshly minted detective badge and an earnestness born of a need to impress her colleagues.

They sat hunched around the conference table in the Newport Police station, on creaky chairs that looked like they would collapse at any minute. They were reviewing the most recent information on a baby recently found in a coal chute in a house on Thames Street. It was an unoccupied house that was being renovated for sale. He first turned his attention to Phil Hudson. "Okay, let's take a look at what we currently have on baby John Doe from the house on Thames Street."

Phil replied, "The house is listed as being owned by Robert and Jessica Arnold. Robert died several years back and Jessica just recently died. The home is currently being renovated for sale and being administered by their son, Robert, Junior. Because of its location on Thames Street in Newport, the renovation is subject to several code enforcements. There is a coal chute that connected the basement to the side of the home that had not been in use for many years. Because of various codes, the opening to the coal chute on the outside of the house could not be removed so the contractor was evaluating the integrity of the chute down to the basement when he made a grisly discovery."

He passed around two of the photographs he had from the scene showing a baby's body in the opening. He took a quick gulp of coffee from his 20 oz. Newport Creamery cup.

"They found a baby's body wrapped in old newspaper, a receiving blanket and dressed in a baptismal dress. As soon as they realized what the blanket contained, they called the police to come and investigate the site. Multiple photographs were taken at the scene along with some specimens and the coroner was then called to come and retrieve the body. The site has been sealed since the initial discovery so that no evidence would be compromised."

Sheila Goldstein was sitting on the other side of Tony. She was trimly dressed, almost severe in comparison to Phil but pleasant in demeanor and she seemed especially deferential to Tony. She then took up the narrative. "The preliminary from the morgue shows that the infant was wrapped in newspapers from around the time of the Challenger disaster in late January of 1986. The receiving blanket appears to have been clean at the time of the burial and it was a new christening outfit that the baby was dressed in. The initial investigation of the body showed no obvious signs of injury. There were some signs of mummification of the baby's skin, probably due to the dry climate inside the coal chute."

They could all see these features in the pictures that Phil had passed around. Sheila continued, "These chutes were designed to keep water out of the basement and were often dry as a bone, even years after being abandoned. The contractor did say that the door into the basement was sealed off and it had to be opened to be able to investigate the inside of the chute.

"After being taken to the morgue, the baby was undressed by the morgue assistant and he noted that there were no outward signs of trauma or lacerations or incisions on the baby. The internal organs had autolysed, making even a preliminary cause of death difficult to discern at this time. A more detailed autopsy will be performed and tissue for DNA sampling will be obtained from the remains. The lab will also look into the possibility that the newspaper was planted to throw off the actual time of the baby's death. The coroner's estimate was that the infant was no more than 3 to 5 days old at the time of its death, but that it had not been stillborn!"

Tony had been listening carefully to his colleagues' information. As the head of this team he was always evaluating their performance. "Good job so far people. There are several obvious directions this investigation needs to take. We'll go over missing person's reports from the general time of early 1986 and look for unusual police reports that were filed during that time. We need to look at the ownership of the house and the tenants that might have been there in the last 25-30 years. Let's also look at contractors that have worked on the house, a job that should be easy in Newport since the regulations make those filings mandatory.

"Phil, tell me about that unusual police report from a physician in Providence that was called in around the week that this baby supposedly was dumped in that coal chute."

"It sounds far-fetched" reported Phil, "but a physician by the name of Jack Del Rio called around that time from the Rhode Island Women's and Infants Hospital in Providence. He reported that he had just operated on a coed from Salve Regina College here in Newport. She claimed she had never been pregnant. His findings were consistent with her having recently delivered a full term baby. The sergeant who took the call basically dismissed it as a crank call and never even recorded her name. I spoke to Dr. Del Rio early last evening and have made arrangements for him to come to the station today to tell his story. Interestingly, although the doctor was surprised by my call, he was not surprised that I was calling about a baby and he never asked if it was dead, how it had died or when."

Tony contemplated this information for a few minutes, "Let me know when he gets here, I'd like to sit in on your conversation with him."

"Sheila," Tony said, "Let's run down the baptismal dress and see if we can find out where it was manufactured and the approximate dating for that type of article. Same thing with the receiving blanket. I'd like to get a handle on this investigation before the press starts making all kinds of crazy and unwarranted accusations. After we get some records on the house, we'll bring the Arnolds in and talk to them about of who was in the house around that time and if any strange occurrences were going on."

"What kind of strange occurrences are we talking about chief?" asked Sheila.

"You know, witchcraft or Satanism," replied Tony.

Phil saw Sheila knit her brow like she had another question but decided to remain quiet; she probably wasn't sure if he was serious or just pulling her leg. She would likely consult with Phil later.

Tony continued to think out loud. "I have been in this job long enough to know that this is not going to be a run-of-the-mill investigation. I am not ready to call this a murder investigation yet but it certainly has all the earmarks to suggest that's what it will become. I hate cases that involve injuries to children and the possible murder of a newborn child is particularly disturbing." He took a sip of the stale coffee in front of him and threw the rest in the trash can. "I need a smoke ... "

Chapter 3

JACK HAD POURED himself a second drink and was watching the late news but realized he hadn't heard a word. His mind wandered back to that night in 1986. Jack remembered how he and Kate got Mary ready for a vaginal scan by letting her go into the bathroom to empty her bladder. She needed assistance as she was a little bit lightheaded and dizzy when she tried to get up. She needed immediate treatment for her bleeding!

After they put her legs up in stirrups, Jack carefully separated her labia to view the opening into her vagina while he continued his running conversation with her to distract her attention from the exam. Jack pointed out to Kate several lacerations along the lateral borders of the vagina in the area where the hymeneal ring had been. Jack continued his conversation with the patient as he carefully placed a speculum in her vaginal canal, removing some blood clots from there. As they inspected a dark and cyanotic cervix, he gave a knowing look to his resident. He calmly asked the patient if she had ever been pregnant and she once again denied that she had ever had a pregnancy. He then introduced the vaginal scan probe covered by a sterile condom and identified the cervix. He documented its thickness and size and he noted that there were remnants of tissue and/or blood clots within the cervical canal.

When they had completed the vaginal scan, they sat Mary up slightly and Jack once again took her hand. "You need a D&C because you have tissue in your cervix that is causing your heavy bleeding. You are not going to stop bleeding until I remove those tissue fragments."

"Go ahead," Mary replied weakly, "the pain is really bad and the heavy bleeding is scaring me."

During this time a repeat blood count showed her to be moderately anemic despite the two units of blood she had received and her white blood cell count suggested that she had an infection. As they prepared her for the operating room, Jack ordered four units of blood to be typed and crossed for her and they started her on triple antibiotics of ampicillin, gentamicin, and clindamycin. He suspected the infection had been brewing for several days and this "shotgun" approach with multiple antibiotics was meant to cover all the bases.

In the operating room, Jack and Kate put Mary up in stirrups. As the D&C began, the bleeding momentarily increased and then slowly trickled off as he removed small chunks of placenta from the uterus with a banjo curette. The tricky part of this procedure was knowing when to stop. He asked the anesthesiologist to add oxytocin to the IV solution. He could feel the fundus of the uterus starting to firm up, coinciding with the decreased bleeding that was coming from the cervical canal.

Jack then turned his attention to the vaginal canal. He re-examined the lacerations near the introitus in the classic position of lacerations caused by an uncontrolled, spontaneous vaginal delivery. None needed suturing. The top of the uterus was now 2 to 3 cm below the level of her umbilicus. The uterus felt firm and the bleeding had subsided substantially. Jack was satisfied that he had removed the fragments from the uterine cavity and cervical canal that had been responsible for her heavy bleeding. She would likely need only one or two more units of blood.

Jack then turned his attention to the fragments of tissue that he had removed from the uterus. He spread them out on a blue towel on the Mayo stand. They looked like typical fragments of a mature placenta. They showed signs of infection. As they transported the patient to the recovery room, he decided that he was going to wait and sit with her until she recovered from her anesthesia. He planned to confront her with the truth of what he had found. He wanted to see if he could persuade her to divulge the full story. Jack realized sadly that before the night was over he might be talking to the local police.

Chapter 4

Tony, Phil and Sheila assembled outside the house on Thames Street where the police tape was still in evidence. From the street, the architecture was classic New England saltbox; rectangular with evenly space windows on the first and second floors. There was a four Gable roof with a chimney protruding on the back gable. The first floor extended out an extra 10-12 feet on the back of the house. It was clear that renovations were going on but there was no construction crew here and the residence was quiet. The street however was pretty busy. They were three or four blocks from the intersection with America's Cup Boulevard, in the heart of the shopping district and multiple tourists stopped and stared at the yellow police tape that designated a crime scene.

Phil took down the police tape, unlocked the front door and they all stepped into the front vestibule and removed their sunglasses. The house was quiet and there was a faint odor but not the decomp that Phil had expected; only wood, plaster, and latex paint. It was warm inside but not as hot as it had been outside. All the rooms were empty and it was obvious construction was going on in the bathroom and kitchen. As they wandered around they saw other obvious construction sites in various rooms where the worker's equipment was strewn about. Once the body had been discovered, there were strict rules that everything was to be left in place. As Tony looked around, he imagined that the workers must have been quite upset to leave their tools behind.

"I hope these guys have another job to do right now and some tools to do it with. Let's see if we can wrap up our investigation here as fast as possible so that we can get them back into this worksite. Let's see if we can confirm that the baby's body has been present in the basement for the last two decades because then we can release the rest of the site."

Phil led them down the stairs to the basement. The furnace was in disarray, obviously being dismantled to be replaced. There was an oil storage tank in the right corner of the basement which had obviously been used to feed this furnace. The setup looked like it was about thirty years old, and there was no evidence of the coal burning furnace that would have been used prior to that time. The door to the coal chute was partially opened and there was yellow tape in abundance all over this area. There was a hammer and chisel on the floor and broken fragments of mortar that had obviously been chipped away from the door so it could be opened.

"Look," said Phil, "there is a slight layer of rust on the mortar and the door that match. It probably formed while the mortar dried after it was put there. This area doesn't look like it's been touched in years." Inside the chute was another story. Here the dust had been disturbed recently. It looked like something had been dragged out of the enclosure. There were several fragments of old yellowed newspaper still visible in the bottom of the chute. Phil pointed his flashlight into the darkness above. The chute rose about 4 to 5 feet to street level and there was a door visible at the top. Surprisingly there were no drafts noticeable in the chute, and no light leaking through the door at the top of the chute. The odor was neutral; not at all what Phil expected if a dead body had been contained in this space for 20 years.

"Sheila," asked Tony, "did you bring the pictures that were taken at the time the body was discovered? "

"Yes, I did." She pulled out a sheaf of forty pictures for them to look at. They were silent for a few minutes as they each looked at and then passed on each picture.

"Sheila," said Phil, "we have only glanced at these before now and I only passed around 2 or 3 of them at the office. Now that you can see them at the scene where they were taken, does anything stand out? What do you see that we might be missing?"

She looked at Phil for a couple seconds, "Well the pictures pretty much tell a story of how this discovery was made. The door was ajar and the mortar fragments on the floor look like the door had not been disturbed before this discovery. The first picture looking into the chute shows the newspaper opened, a receiving blanket pulled back just enough to see the face of the baby with a hat on. There seemed to be some old crinkled cellophane near the newspaper. The pictures then document the body being removed from the chute and placed on a table nearby with the newspaper carefully being collected. One shot of the headlines of the newspaper clearly showed the classic picture of the Challenger explosion with the two solid rocket boosters going off in different directions. More of the blanket was unraveled showing the baby to be dressed in what looks like a baptismal outfit, including a bonnet and booties. The face was shriveled and does not look doll like, more like the mummies you see in a museum. It looks like they were afraid to disturb the body because they did not undress it at that time. The last picture documents that the coroner had taken possession of the body."

"Can you guys think of anything else we need to do at this

crime scene?" asked Tony. "It looks like these pictures have pretty well documented exactly what we need to know. Samples have been taken and brought to the lab for analysis and the coroner will be able to continue working on the autopsy. It looks like we have the appropriate timeline for what happened here and we can now release this crime scene. Let's get back to the office so we can start looking over other the pieces of information we've been able to gather so far."

As they climbed the stairs from the basement Sheila took one more look around and shuddered. "I wonder what happened here?" she said softly, mostly to herself.

Chapter 5

J ACK SAT NEXT TO Mary's stretcher in the recovery room. He watched her chest rise and fall with her breathing. He had given her two units of blood and her color was improving and her respiratory rate was slowing to normal. Her pulse rate was also slowing now to the low 100s and her blood pressure was stable. Her temperature still ran a little bit over 102°F.

He had sat almost motionless by her side for the last 35 minutes. The recovery room nurse kept checking on her as required and exchanged furtive glances with him. She was confused about his presence because most doctors did not wait in the recovery room for their patients to wake up. He had been listening to the beeping of various monitors and IV infusion pumps as well as respirators that reminded him of Darth Vader since that character had burst onto the national scene.

Finally, Mary Murphy's eyelids fluttered gently and she slowly opened her eyes and looked around. It took her a few minutes before she managed to focus her eyes on him. Jack slowly rose to his feet and took her hand into his. "We need to talk." She looked away from him. "You have been lying to me. After 8 years of delivering babies, I know that your story of having never been pregnant is not true. You have delivered a baby in the last few days and the placenta never came out, that's why you have been bleeding heavily and got infected."

"It's not true, I have never been pregnant," said Mary very softly. He told her that he had specimens sent to the pathology department that would soon confirm that she had mature placental fragments that he had removed from her uterus. This would confirm that she had recently delivered a full term pregnancy. She shook her head in bewilderment and once again reiterated that she had never been pregnant.

"You can stick to that story if you want to but I am sure that you have recently given birth. I am your doctor and I will keep taking care of you no matter what but right now I am concerned about your baby!" After her initial deflation, Jack could see fear starting to creep into her eyes.

"The week before this last period started, during one of my trips to the bathroom, I realized that a large clot had fallen out into the toilet bowl. It scared me and I quickly flushed it down the toilet." The words burst out of her like a torrent. Jack guessed that she figured if she said it loudly and quickly he would have to believe her. Instead, it made her less believable.

Once again he expressed his doubts about the story because the size baby that would be required to cause the tears to her cervix and vaginal canal was not consistent with an early pregnancy loss that would be small enough to be flushed down the toilet. He saw defiance rising now.

"I have never been pregnant!"

He decided he would try a new tactic. He told her that she'd bled very heavily for the past several days and required two units of blood here as well as the two units at Newport Hospital. She had obviously become infected and was now on antibiotics to make that infection subside. He told her the worst was over but she would need to recover for a few more days. He told her to expect some abdominal tenderness and period like cramping.

"I do have belly tenderness and I can feel the cramps. They do seem better than they did before the surgery. "

"That's good," he assured her. "Over the next few days the tenderness will get better but the cramps will continue and that is good news because it will minimize your bleeding." She was starting to calm down. He told her she should expect to remain hospitalized for about two more days with IV antibiotics and that if she improved enough during that period of time, she would then be sent home on oral antibiotics. She seemed relieved not to be talking about pregnancy anymore and he didn't have the heart to go back to that part of the conversation. He needed to get back to his call room so he could mull over the situation.

Jack sat in his call room and decided that he would proceed with the next step. The room was even drabber now than he remembered from just a few hours ago. He had been thinking a great deal about what he should do while he waited for Mary to wake up. His first inclination to confront her in the recovery room had not worked out as he expected. He had hoped she would account for the baby's whereabouts. He took a breath, picked up the phone and called his Chairman of Obstetrics and Gynecology at Rhode Island Women's and Infants Hospital. He outlined what had occurred so far during the evening and expressed his concern that there was a baby somewhere out there in jeopardy on this cold, late January day. They discussed several scenarios about what might have occurred, not one of them had a good ending. Jack was concerned that she had abandoned the baby somewhere in the Newport area or that the baby had come to some kind of tragic end. After several more minutes of discussion with his chief, he made the fateful decision. He was going to call the police on his patient.

Chapter 6

DETECTIVE TONY FUENTES cleared his desk of other files and waved Phil and Sheila into his office. They walked into his office in single file, Phil slightly disheveled as usual but with some well organized file notes under his arm, and Sheila tastefully dressed in a navy blue skirt, white blouse and running shoes. Tony looked at her feet quizzically. "Boss, you never know when you have to run somewhere," said Sheila. "I found out last week that running after a suspect in pumps doesn't work!" Tony smiled as he remembered the story.

"Okay people," said Tony, "let's review what we found so far. Sheila, tell us what you found out about the tenants at the Thames Street house."

"I ran that address through DMV and got multiple hits on driving licenses registered to that home," said Sheila. "Looks like there's at least nine or 10 names on the list, one or two at a time for 6 to 7 years in different stretches. I cross-referenced that list with warrants and convictions and only one or two names popped up. One was for domestic violence calls but there were no allegations of any child abuse even though some of the kids in the house were not his. There was another conviction on check kiting for someone who was trying to help his mother pay off medical bills after her insurance expired. He got a suspended sentence with parole and has not resurfaced in the system again."

"Sheila, go back 20 to 25 years and check to see if there were any young kids or teenagers in the house at that time that might have had some complaints about abusing animals," said Tony. Sheila nodded her head as she took notes in her spiral binder. "What about you Phil. Do you have anything else to report at this time?"

"While Sheila was looking at the tenants in the house, I looked around that neighborhood for anyone who might have been charged or convicted of child abuse or child molestation. Every time I do this I am shocked to find that no matter what neighborhood I look at, there are usually two or three suspect names of registered sex offenders. The system was not as efficient back then as it is now but I came up with three names worth looking into. Jim Bonhomme lived two streets over from the Thames Street address and in 1982 he was convicted of kidnapping and murdering three young teenage girls. None of them were from the Newport community and there was no evidence that he ever had any interest in young children. He got 35 years to life and is still at the ACI in Cranston. I'll take a ride up there and interview him to see if he knows of any names that did not make my suspect list."

"What makes you think he will talk to you?" asked Sheila.

"Oh, he'll talk to me but he will probably tell me all kinds of lies that will chase me all over the city, getting nowhere. He'll want something first, so I will check with the guards to see if he'll want cigarettes or more TV privileges."

"What about the other two names?" asked Tony.

"The next name on my list is Jason Somerville. He comes from a wealthy family in the Newport Casino/Tennis Hall of

Fame neighborhood, 5 to 6 blocks from Thames Street. As you suggested to Sheila, he had multiple run-ins with the law as a child with neighbors complaining of missing pets in the neighborhood. Nothing ever got pinned on him but later in his life there were multiple allegations of domestic violence from his young male partners. Most of those charges were dropped and the police felt that the victims had been paid off by the family. I looked through his extensive file and never found anything suggesting he had anything to do with children but maybe had a brief period of time with that before he moved on to the young teenage boys."

Sheila squirmed in her chair and said, "I thought the two years I worked vice were as low as I would ever get but this is going to get really ugly isn't it?"

Tony took off his reading glasses and threw them on the chart in front of him. "Vice is a different kind of job, Sheila. Unsavory as it seems, you get to meet the same people over and over and after a while you see they do have some redeeming traits. Homicide is totally different, especially when you're dealing with the death of a child. It gets harder and harder to see any humanity in the people that are perpetrating these crimes. You may ultimately find that you don't have the stomach for it but I think you're doing fine right now." He turned his attention back to Phil who was nodding his head in agreement. "Phil, did you say you had a third suspect?"

"Yes I did boss, but actually I haven't finished with Jason yet. Jason is now the CFO of his family's company and his recent dossier is empty. He seems to have settled down with one partner and if we are going to get close to him, I think we're going to have to go through an army of lawyers. Hopefully he will have a solid alibi for that month of January in 1986 and then we can cross his name off this list.

"The third suspect is a woman named Harriet Jones. She evidently couldn't have children of her own and in 1983 she was caught trying to steal a baby from the nursery at the hospital. She never even got off the hospital grounds so she served two years in jail and then five years probation. She checked in with her parole officer on a monthly basis during that five years and a year later she relocated to Southern California and no one knows where she's been for the last 16 years. I think the FBI has a unit I can contact that helps find people who were implicated in kidnappings in the past. I'll make a few calls."

Chapter 7

JACK TOOK ANOTHER SIP of his whiskey and his mind
drifted back to that early morning in the call room. Jack had
picked up the phone and dialed the hospital operator. "Hi, this is
Dr. Del Rio. Could you please connect me to the on-call hospital
attorney?" He had actually been surprised to realize that there
was a house attorney on call for the hospital at all times but after
he thought about it for a minute, it made perfect sense.

"Hello, this is Bob Newhouse, how can I help you?" The voice
sounded sleepy to Jack, obviously Bob was not someone who was
used to taking calls in the middle of night.

"Bob, this is Dr. Jack Del Rio. I have a situation going on here
at the hospital that I need your advice on."

"You don't think this is something that could've waited till
the morning?" asked an obviously irritated Bob.

"Well, if the patient leaves the hospital Against Medical
Advice before morning, we will have lost our opportunity to call
the police on her," said Jack.

"Okay, you now have my full attention. What's up?"

"I had a patient transferred to me from the Newport Hospital
for heavy vaginal bleeding. To make a long story short, I took her
to the operating room to do a D&C on her and I have concluded
that she has delivered a baby in the last few days. The problem is

she denies ever having been pregnant. My problem is that I am concerned that there is a baby out there somewhere that could be in jeopardy. I know that patient confidentiality is usually paramount but in this case we may be able to save a baby."

"I see," said Mr. Newhouse. "Let me think for a minute." Jack lay back on the creaky bed, listening to silence for 30 seconds. "How hard did you try to find out what happened to the baby?"

"I tried real hard," said Jack. "I provided her with at least three pieces of evidence to prove to her that I know that she had recently given birth to a baby. Despite that, she repeatedly denied ever being pregnant and became more emphatic with each pronouncement."

"Well Dr. Del Rio, I think under the circumstances we have little choice but to alert the authorities."

"I was afraid you would say that, I'll give the Providence Police a call. I'll let you know what happens."

"In the morning, if you please." Jack hung up and redialed the operator.

"Hi, this is Dr. Del Rio again. Could you connect me to the local precinct of the Providence Police Department please?"

"Doctor, I get a lot of strange requests in an overnight shift but this is a first for me. Give me a minute to look up the number."

"Angela, this is a first for me too, thanks for your help."

"Hello, this is Sgt. Bill O'Malley, how can I help you?"

Jack remembered thinking baritone voice, big guy, lifetime cop, slight Boston accent. "Sgt., I don't even know where to begin."

"You could start by telling me your name."

"Oh, sorry, this is Dr. Jack Del Rio at Rhode Island Hospital. I'm a little nervous because I've never done this before."

"You never called the police before, you never reported a crime before, or you've never committed a crime before?"

"I've never reported a patient to the police before."

"That's going to be a first for me too doctor, go slowly and I'm sure you and I can make it through this together."

Just what I need, thought Jack, a sarcastic cop. He started from the beginning, outlining the case as he had for the hospital attorney but filling in a few more pertinent facts. To his credit, Sgt. O'Malley listened quietly until Jack was finished. Jack realized he had hardly taken a breath during his narrative.

"That's a fascinating story Doctor. So, your worry is that this patient may have abandoned or disposed of her baby. Maybe the baby is with her parents or her boyfriend. Did you ask her about that?"

"No, I didn't ask that explicitly because she continuously denied she had ever been pregnant!" Jack knew that this was an unusual story but he was getting irritated by Sgt. O'Malley's attitude.

"Doctor, you said that this patient was transferred to you from Newport is that right?"

"Yes, that is correct," said Jack.

"So the suggestion is that she probably gave birth in Newport, and if she disposed of or abandoned the baby, it would probably be in their jurisdiction."

"So you're telling me that you're not interested in following up on this case, is that right?" asked Jack.

"Pretty much," said Sgt. O'Malley. "From your description doctor, I don't think a crime has been committed in Providence. I definitely think you should contact the Newport police."

"Okay," said Jack dejectedly. "But before we end this call, could you please give me your name, badge number and precinct supervisor's name?"

"No problem," said Sgt. O'Malley, and he provided Jack with the information requested.

Jack hung up and closed his eyes for a few minutes. He opened up his eyes and slowly looked around the drab call room. There was a small TV in the corner. The cot that he slept on had white sheets, a threadbare blanket and single pillow. There was one sitting chair, a desk and a small lamp on the desk. Jack covered for the university group on average once every 10 days and felt confined to this cubicle for 24 hours at a time. He had come to look at these days as a loss to his lifetime. He realized that he did important work and that his teaching of medical students and residents was critical to their development.

He was now mentally and physically exhausted and had already made a call to his chairman, the hospital attorney and the Providence police and was still nowhere. He picked up the phone to call the operator again.

"Hi Jack," said Angela. "How can I help you now?"

"I want you to connect me to the Newport Police Department."

"Of course you do," said Angela.

"Please Angela; I don't need you to get sarcastic with me too! Could you please just connect me?" She did.

Jack spoke to the desk sergeant in Newport. As he expected, the conversation took on the familiar tone of the call with the Providence police. The conclusion was similar.

"So doctor, you're calling me from Rhode Island Hospital in Providence, is that right?"

"That is correct," said Jack, "and you're going to tell me that it is their jurisdiction, dammit! But before you hang up could you please give me your full name, rank, badge number and supervisor's name?" The sergeant did so and Jack wrote it all down on the same pad with the info from Sgt O'Malley so he could put it in the patient's chart in the morning.

Jack called the operator one more time. She was no longer sarcastic and just connected him to Bob Newhouse as requested. Jack explained the phone calls to the Providence and Newport police and told Bob that he felt he should call child protective services. Bob agreed with him. Jack called the child protective services advocate who was on call for the hospital in that early morning. He once again outlined the details of the case. When he was done, the advocate asked him if he had a baby that was being abused. Jack was furious. "There is no baby, that's the problem!"

"Doctor, when you find the baby that's being abused, please call us back," the advocate had replied to him. Jack once again concluded this phone call by asking for her name and her supervisor's information. Jack's head was now swimming; you were mandated by law to report potential child abuse but evidently that did not mean the agency or the police had to investigate the incident.

The next few days had flown by for Jack. He took care of Mary as he would any other patient that had required a post delivery D&C. Her red blood cell counts remained stable, her fever subsided, and her white blood cell count went back to normal. He discharged her on the third postoperative day on oral antibiotics. As expected, she had never returned for her post operative check. He had decided during this period of time that his job was going to continue to be a doctor and that clearly no one wanted him to be a policeman, detective, or child advocate. After several more sleepless nights he decided that the best case scenario would be that she had given the baby up for adoption to a wealthy couple for a large sum of money. She had seemed to be a very intelligent young lady. It was another few weeks before he stopped looking in the paper for a headline about a dead baby found in Newport.

Twenty years later, the phone call had come.

Chapter 8

JACK SAT IN A POLICE interview chair for the first time ever where he was the focus of the conversation. He looked around the room. It looked like a typical precinct interrogation room from the many detective TV shows he had watched over the years. There was little light filtering in through the high window and he could tell that it was late in the day. There was a large mirror covering one wall which was likely two-way. The table had a place to secure handcuffs. The chairs were metal with most of the paint worn off from continuous use. He had already waited for several minutes and was getting nervous. He was hoping to make it out of there before sundown.

Detectives Philip Hudson and Sheila Goldstein entered the interrogation room together. They explained that the detective in charge, Antonio Fuentes had had to leave for a family commitment and that they would conduct this interview.

"I'm sorry I'm late," said Jack. "I was caught up at the clinic and the last patient was more complicated than I expected. There are some things you just can't rush and that's I why got here later than expected."

"We completely understand, doctor," said Phil, "we just have some preliminary questions for you today. Could you please outline for us, to your best recollection, what transpired on the day you called the Newport Police Department in January of 1986."

"I have given it some thought since you called yesterday," said Jack. He went on to recite as closely as he could the conversations he'd had with the Providence police, the Newport police and the child protective services in Providence.

"Sounds like you had a frustrating but memorable day," commented Phil. "Did I just hear you say that you talked to the Providence police and Child protective services that night? We did not know that."

"I sure did! It was a frustrating day, night, and middle of the night." said Jack. "I have never spent more time talking to policemen then I did that night. It was particularly frustrating since I felt I had to break my patient's confidentiality to report a possible case of child abuse. After wrestling with my conscience, it turns out no one was particularly interested in hearing my story."

"We are definitely interested in hearing your story now, doctor," said Phil.

"Seems like it's a little too little and a little too late…like 20 years too late!" said Jack.

"Listen, doctor," said Phil, "we can only handle things as they are at the present time. Could you please elaborate on the fact that you thought the cover story that resulted in transferring the patient to your hospital in Providence was a lie?"

"Well," said Jack," I knew the transferring doctor pretty well. He'd always been lazy and liked to transfer problem patients out of his care. He really just expected me to accept his version of the story. The gist of the story just didn't make sense to me. Heavy bleeding and an enlarged uterus in a teenage patient were much more likely to be associated with a pregnancy than a fibroid.

Fibroids are rather uncommon in a teenage patient and they seldom presented as an episode of heavy bleeding."

"Do you think he actually knew what was wrong with his patient?" asked Phil.

"I'm sure he knew what was going on," said Jack, "I said he was lazy but he wasn't stupid. He just thought transferring the patient to me was a way to avoid taking care of her."

"Do you think he knew this patient prior to this episode?" asked Phil.

"No," said Jack, "I didn't get the idea that he knew this patient before this episode. I think he just got called to see her because he was covering the emergency room in Newport that night."

"Do you think he thought there was some criminal activity associated with this patient?" asked Phil

"No, I didn't get that idea either," said Jack. "I'm not sure he thought it through that far. He was just happy I was going to take her off his hands."

"Did you know this patient prior to that night?" asked Sheila.

"No, I only met her that night in the emergency room because I was covering the University group," said Jack.

"Do you think she acted like a criminal when you met her in the emergency room, doctor?" asked Sheila.

"No, she acted like a scared little girl which is what she was."

"Did she act guilty when you confronted her in the recovery room?" asked Sheila.

"I'm not sure which way you mean guilty," said Jack. "She seemed guilty of having kept a secret for a long time which was now going to be revealed."

"You mean the pregnancy"

"Yes, the pregnancy"

"Did she tell you her name herself?"

"Yes, she said her name was Mary Murphy but that ended up being a lie also."

"Wait a minute," interrupted Phil. "How do you know that?"

"Because that's how I got into trouble with this transfer," said Jack. "I discharged her from the hospital on the second day after the D&C with some antibiotics to take home. The next day the hospital billing center called me and told me that her insurance information was incorrect. They berated me for having accepted her without conferring with the Transfer Center of the hospital. The Transfer Center was designed to stop these kinds of episodes from occurring." Jack went on to explain that he often accepted patients without proper authority from the Transfer Center. He accepted them under what he called "the rule of the teenager." Jack smiled at them and said, "You know, you can do almost anything once by pleading ignorance." Phil and Sheila squirmed in their chairs. Jack smiled again and continued, "The other variation of that scroll was that it is easier to ask for forgiveness than it is to ask for permission." He saw them roll their eyes at each other and decided they must think he was being a smartass. He liked that! Jack explained that he was unhappy with the Transfer Center because it would occasionally let a baby transfer to Rhode Island Hospital with a critical cardiac defect but not allow the mother to transfer. The baby ended up at one hospital in critical condition and the mother ended up at the outlying hospital, having had a cesarean section and with no ability to rejoin her dying newborn. Jack felt it was cruel to not reunite this mother-baby pair just so the hospital could save money. Jack explained that although he had violated the rule several times during his career, this was the only time he'd been called on it. "So I suspect you will not find a Mary Murphy at Salve Regina College."

"This makes the episode very suspicious," said Phil. "Did you tell the hospital authorities about your suspicion from the day of surgery?"

"No," said Jack. "I just mumbled my apologies and took my medicine. I'm not sure you understand how traumatic this episode was for me. On the day of her admission and surgery I had violated patient confidentiality and gotten nothing for my effort! I had no interest in repeating that again. I told you before, I had learned my lesson; I was just going to be a doctor and not a policeman anymore."

Sheila noted how agitated Phil was becoming. "We are done with questions for now Dr. Del Rio." She glanced at Phil and he nodded his head in agreement and Jack got up and left.

Sheila and Phil sat in stunned silence for a few minutes after Jack had left. When they were sure he was no longer able to hear them, they both started talking at once.

"I think we are on the right track," said Sheila.

"This sounds very suspicious," said Phil. "It sure looks out like this is going to end up being related to this baby we just found. The doctor seemed pretty forthcoming with his comments. This was obviously a traumatic event for him. If you read the transcript from the duty officer from that night and you listen to his account today, they are almost identical. I am surprised that after this long he could remember that episode in such great detail. At first it was so exact, I thought it might have rehearsed it over and over in his head, but he did seem genuine in how he presented it."

"I agree," said Sheila. "I think we got some real information to follow-up on. I'll get the transcript from the Providence police and see if I can run down the chart with the Child Care Advocate's information. The hospital chart might give us clues to the girl's identity even if she wasn't Mary Murphy."

"Tony is going to be very upset he wasn't here for this interview!" observed Phil.

Chapter 9

JACK STRODE PURPOSEFULLY out of the Newport Police Department. He was feeling guilty. He wasn't sure why he was feeling guilty. He wasn't sure if it was because he had recounted a betrayal of his patient's trust. He wasn't sure if he felt guilty that he hadn't been forceful enough for the investigation to proceed 20 years ago. He wasn't sure if it was his concern that recounting the story now was going to result in that young woman's life being turned upside down once again. As the years had passed he realized that she would have put this episode further and further into her past. Now it was going to be dredged up again. He knew that wasn't his fault; it was the recent discovery of this baby that had precipitated these events. Still, that didn't make him feel any better.

He was surprised at how easily he had returned to the mindset of that night. Phil and Sheila had been very good at extracting the story from him. Thankfully, Sheila had ended the session because Phil was obviously getting upset with him. He wondered if she would get into trouble because of that. He had expected them to question him on his care of the patient for the two days after the surgery. He suspected Phil would have been even more upset when he told them that he had just taken care of her as he would have taken care of any patient who had undergone the ordeal she had undergone. Phil would also be upset when he heard about the patient's college friends who had left hurriedly after the recovery room exchange, never to return to the hospital. Sheila probably hadn't wanted her partner to continue asking questions while he was upset. Jack was sure he would hear from them again and he would continue telling them the other events he could remember from that three-day period in 1986. The events were taking on even more clarity as he thought more about that night.

Jack carefully wound his car onto the entrance ramp to the Newport Bridge by the old Jai Alai Fronton in Newport. He had been right that this was going to be perfect timing as he drove up the access to the bridge. He could see the setting sun framed in the archways of the bridge. It was a magnificent sight at this time of twilight, and this view always took Jack's breath away. He looked to the right at the Naval War College. He glanced towards the left but couldn't quite make out Goat Island and the innumerable boats docked in Newport Harbor. His eye followed the north/south route of the East passage of Narragansett Bay as it made its way past Jamestown. He continued west on 138, crossing through Jamestown and then crossed the new Jamestown-Verrazano Bridge over the west passage of Narragansett Bay. He turned south on Route 1, went past the exit for RI 108 and then turned to skirt the west side of the Salt Pond, down Succotash Road, making his way into Snug Harbor. He laughed as he remembered the first time he went all the way to the end of the road and ended across the inlet to the Marina. So near but so far away! That night he had to turn back and retrace his steps to the turnoff. It was just sunset as he parked his car.

He carried a small bag of groceries across the dock and onto his boat. He felt more relaxed as soon as he walked onto the deck that was pitching slightly. There was a minimal amount of chop present on the water this night. He slipped into the small galley and poured himself two fingers of single malt scotch and he turned on the grill. He unpacked the small steak he had picked up for dinner, adorned it with some steak sauce and put it on the grill. He threw a small potato into the microwave to bake. He felt the tension of the day continue to melt away. He sipped his scotch and watched the steak cook. He considered that one of the worst residuals of his two failed marriages was that he would eat dinner alone tonight. In general he welcomed solitude, especially after the busy day he had at the clinic today, but he still hated eating alone. Tomorrow would be Friday and at least he could be happy in the thought that Sally would join him for the weekend.

Sally Hamel was his girlfriend. They had settled into a comfortable routine. She was a few years younger than Jack and had no children. She taught Ancient History at the Norwich Military Academy in Vermont. It was too far away for them to meet on a daily basis and it was still a mystery to him why this long distance relationship worked out so well. Still, this relationship had been going on for 15 years, longer than both of his marriages together. He still stayed overnight in Providence once in a while and often called on various friends to have dinner with. They occasionally even stayed the night with him after dinner. None of those relationships had ever seriously compromised his arrangement with Sally. They were completely committed to each other on weekends and vacations. He had failed to achieve a committed relationship in either of his marriages.

Jack also sometimes visited his son, Jack Junior, and his family in Cranston, Rhode Island. He missed the days when he and Jack Junior spent quality time with each other. But Jack Junior's family was flourishing and he seemed to have a strong marriage. Jack was happy about that turn of events. He enjoyed the visits of his two young grandchildren. Jack Junior had turned his life around from a troubled youth and Jack was proud of that fact.

Jack wondered if he should let Jack Junior in on the current situation about the mysterious patient he had taken care of in 1986. Jack had previously told no one in his family about the odyssey he'd been on that night. Jack did not usually talk about work to either of his wives or to Jack Junior. Neither of his wives appreciated that trait, especially when he was out later than expected or came home at odd hours. Jack had always felt that patient confidentiality was paramount, especially in a job like gynecology. Each wife had been surprised when she met old friends who were three or four months pregnant. The friends had likewise been surprised that even after two or three visits with Jack, his wife still didn't know about their pregnancy. Jack had always felt that each patient had the right to inform friends of their pregnancies on their own terms. Each wife had ultimately become suspicious of his reason for remaining away. Of course each wife had ultimately been correct that some of his time away had been extracurricular and not professional. Jack Junior, however, had been happily ignorant of his dad's professional and not so professional life. Later in life, Jack Junior was even happier to realize that Jack had spared him dinnertime talks about vaginas and bleeding.

After dinner and cleanup, Jack sat in his favorite chair and reviewed some medical journals with one eye on the TV. He was actually getting more reading done while watching the Boston Red Sox languish through another late summer season. For the hundredth time he remembered the quotation from Bart Giamatti that being a Red Sox fan taught you about true life; "you blossom in the spring, flourish all summer and then die in the fall." He remembered how great it'd been to watch the Red Sox win the

World Series in 2004 in his dad's house. His dad, with tears in his eyes, had said he never expected to see it in his lifetime. Dad had died a year later. Jack suddenly felt very old. He finished his scotch and went to bed.

Chapter 10

IT WAS EARLY AFTERNOON but the detective squad room had never even slowed down for lunch.

"Okay let's see where we stand," said Tony. Sheila and Phil shuffled through their notes.

"Tony," said Sheila, "have you had a chance to look at the transcripts of the interview we had with Dr. Del Rio?"

"Yes I have, very impressive interview!"

"Phil and I are pretty sure that this is the guy that will get us rolling on this case. The timeline seems to fit very well with timing of the baby's burial."

"I agree," said Tony, "sounds like this girl was having a bad week. We need to find out if anyone else was with her. Did anyone go with her from Newport? Who picked her up from the hospital and brought her home? It would be hard to believe she went through all this turmoil by herself. Besides, when would she have had time to dispose of the baby while she was that sick? What was her connection to the house on Thames Street? We need to get over to Salve Regina College and see if we can track down who she is. Sheila, when we finish this meeting, go over there and see if you can find out who she was and who she was involved with. Phil, what have you found out about the house on Thames Street?"

Phil started, "The house has been in the hands of the Arnold family for 40 years. They initially lived in the house for 14 to 15 years and since then it has been rented out to various people for 5 to 8 years at a time. I have most of the names of the people who rented the house and the list coincides well with the list we got from DMV. Besides the ones Sheila told us about, none of them have any criminal records. I've spoken on the phone to Robert Junior on several occasions and he had his attorney send over the records. He and his wife currently reside in Mystic, Connecticut. Needless to say, they were shocked at this finding. Sheila and I were going to ride out to interview him and his wife, but they volunteered to stop by the station this afternoon after finishing up with some business in Providence."

Sheila then continued, "We tracked down some information on the receiving blanket and baptismal outfit. They were pretty generic and were sold in multiple stores in Rhode Island at that time. Most of those stores kept no records to whom this type of item was sold to. Even with some of the newer technologies, it doesn't look like we're going to get any fingerprints off these items. Likewise, the newspaper was too crumbly to expect to get any fingerprints from it. It looks like that's going to be a dead end, too. Having said all that, it does look like the timeline in early 1986 will hold up."

"We have a preliminary report from the coroner," said Phil. "The coroner thinks the time of death was right around the time of the newspaper article. He thinks that this baby was born alive but was not more than 3 to 4 days old at its death. His reasoning is that it looks like the umbilical cord had just detached from the abdomen of the baby. He has not been able to pin down a cause of death at this time. Most of the internal organs like the brain, lungs, and the liver have disintegrated beyond recognition. There is a small defect in the posterior part of the skull but he can't tell if it was from a traumatic event. He'll continue to look for tools or weapons that might have made that defect. He has sent off some tissue samples which may be helpful when they become available. They will be run for toxicology and infection testing. He thinks he may be able to recover some DNA samples from the body. He is sending the baby's heart out to an expert because baby heart problems are hard enough to diagnose without the deterioration present in this sample. He is preparing some tissue slides for evaluation in the next few days. He can't rule out suffocation as a cause of death. He also can't rule out shaken baby syndrome. Some kind of chemical imbalance or a SIDS death is also possible in these circumstances."

"Clear as mud," declared a disgusted Tony. Tony's phone rang and he answered it. "Listen, the front desk just told me that Mr. Arnold has arrived. Phil, you and I will interview him and Sheila can go off to the college."

Chapter 11

TONY AND PHIL ESCORTED Mr. Arnold into interview room number one. He looked to be in his early 40's and was dressed in a very expensive suit, gold Philippe Patek watch on his wrist and a simple wedding band on his finger. He was alone, no wife or attorney.

"Sorry to have to talk you into a room like this," said Tony. "This is the only place here to get any privacy."

"I understand," said Robert Arnold, Junior. "What can I help you with today? Did you get the records you requested from my attorney?"

"Why don't you just tell us a little bit about what your relationship to this house has been and yes we did get the records from your attorney, thank you," said Tony.

"Well," said Robert Junior, "I lived there for a few years with my parents until I got married and moved out to my own home. That was shortly before my parents moved out of the home to go to a bigger house in Newport. They moved in 1984. It's hard to believe they found a baby in that old coal chute. When my family bought the house, the chute was already closed off. I used to play in that basement as a child but never thought twice about that area because we stayed away from the furnace. After my parents moved out, several couples, most with children, rented the house over the next 15 to 20 years. I knew most of them because I would stop by the house for my dad when he was out of town on business. I helped collect rents and organize work parties to repair various things that broke down over the years. I don't remember any troublemakers renting the house during all those years. I understand that you think the body was put there several years after my parents moved out and the first couple that rented the house had no children during that time."

"What can you tell me about workers or contractors that might have keys to the property?" asked Phil. He fidgeted with a paper clip and Tony smiled at his professional demeanor and schoolboy play with the clip.

"My family had some domestic help when we lived at the house. They would have had keys to the house. I am not sure that any of the people who rented it had any help like we did. My dad changed the locks when he moved out so that anyone we had given the keys to would no longer have access to the house. My dad did arrange that if any of the tenants changed the locks, he would be given a set of keys as the landlord. There may have been contractors who had access to the house and the meter readers for water and electricity would have been allowed in the basement at various times. It is still hard to believe that anyone would put a baby's body in that location."

"We were wondering if anyone who had access to the house would have been involved in drug use, witchcraft or sorcery," asked Phil.

"Wow," said Robert Junior, "I'm not sure what you mean by that. As far as I know we had no tenants that practiced any strange religions and we didn't have anyone that abused their children. There was occasionally a police report suggesting domestic violence but no one was ever formally charged. I think someone was arrested for writing checks with inadequate funds but we never got a bad check from them."

"I thought your wife would be with you," said Phil. "I wonder if you could ask her if she remembered anybody that behaved strangely."

"I'm sorry," said Robert Junior. "When we spoke on the phone I thought Suzanne was coming today but she did not feel well and did not accompany me to Providence. She would not have had much reason to meet any of the tenants of the house. I knew some of them because I helped my dad as I already explained. I will certainly ask her if she knows any of the people who were tenants and whether she felt they had any unusual social characteristics."

"That would be great," said Phil. "I find that sometimes women have better intuition about these behaviors than men do."

"Well," said Tony, "you have been very helpful today and I want to thank you for coming in to help us with this case."

"Please let me know about any more information I can get you," said Robert Junior. "My wife and I would certainly like to find out what's going on here, both for our own piece of mind and because we know what this kind of story can do to a house that's for sale." They all shook hands as Robert Junior get up to leave.

Tony and Phil took a few minutes to finish organizing their notes. "That was not as helpful as I would've liked," said Phil. "It sounds like we have a lot of leads that are going to go nowhere. Curious that Mr. Arnold talked about child abuse, we never mentioned that."

Tony thought about that for a minute, "No, that did not surprise me. I think a lot of people think about child abuse when they hear of a child's death."

Chapter 12

J ACK HEARD THE THROATY ROAR of Sally's Porsche Cayenne Turbo pulling into the parking lot of the Marina. He was sitting on the fantail of his boat watching the last dregs of sunshine disappear into the trees to the west. He was apprehensive on these Friday nights when Sally drove all the way from Vermont to meet him. At least it was still summer time and he didn't have to worry about Sally driving in bad weather. She had noticed his discomfort about her drive in the winter; he recalled the conversation. "How come you drive to Vermont so often during the winter, while I drive to RI in the summer?"

"I drive to Vermont in the winter so we can ski and you should drive to Rhode Island in the summer so we can spend time on the boat," was his retort.

"So it's not because you think I drive too fast in bad weather?" She had accused him of being chauvinistic on more than one occasion.

"Of course not, you drive too fast in good weather, too. And besides, you just bought a car that's too powerful for you!"

Jack watched as Sally Hamel confidently walked up the gangplank to his boat wearing her white cotton summer dress, almost translucent when backlit by the sun. She wore heelless driving shoes that de-emphasized her 5 foot, 10 inch, lithe frame and she had an Adidas overnight bag slung over her shoulder. He thought, as he usually did, how seductive her walk was as she approached him on the deck. As they embraced on the deck, Sally let her overnight bag slip to the deck. Jack held her tightly, stooping over slightly to bury his head in her shoulder. He loved the smell of her. He loved the scent of her shampoo in her hair, the fragrance of perfume on her neck. It amazed him how fresh she always seemed despite the three and half hour ride from Vermont down to Rhode Island. As their embrace broke up, they kissed and sat in chairs with their knees touching. An outside observer would not be able to tell if they were teenagers who had just met and instantly connected with each other or an old couple happy to be reacquainted after a long absence. Jack handed her a glass of Old Vine Zinfandel at a cooler temperature than most experts recommended for red wine. He picked up his glass of single malt scotch and they toasted each other without a word. Each had a twinkle in their eyes.

After 30 seconds of silence, Jack broke the reverie, "so how was your week?"

"I had a great week, we had a faculty workshop and discussed several new teaching techniques, one of which you had explained to me last week. Don't let this go to your head, but everybody thought it was a great idea."

"You mean the one about teaching about the rate limiting step by having consecutive students make the folds for a paper airplane and having one student responsible for printing US Air Force on the wing? Since making the folds is faster than printing, the printing becomes the rate limiting step. But if you keep adding students to the printing job, something else becomes the rate limiting step. "

"No, not that one, although they did like it, too. I mean the lesson about simple diffusion in which you separate a classroom by a row of desks and have everybody on one side with pink T-shirts and everybody on the other side with blue T-shirts. If they start moving around at random and then you open slots in the wall of desks, they soon start mixing and after a while there a similar numbers of pink and blue T-shirts on each side of the divider. Entropy demonstrated instead of described!"

"So they actually like two of my ideas." Jack smirked at her. "Did you explain to them that if you station someone at each open slot who preferentially helps only one color of T-shirts cross in one direction only, you can have one color move against its concentration gradient? Active transport demonstrated!" Jack could hardly conceal his excitement.

"Yes I did," confessed Sally. "And even though I didn't understand what that meant, the science people were really excited." Jack looked positively triumphant! Sally sighed. "So how was your week?"

Jack detailed the stories of some patients he'd seen at the clinic. He described how some patients were making progress; some were not while others were actually going backwards. He wondered aloud for the thousandth time why patients went to the doctor, paid their money and then completely ignored the doctor's advice. Since his current clients visited him at a free clinic, maybe it was more understandable than usual that they ignored his advice. They hadn't paid money out of their own pocket to get that advice. He wondered if most patients who got free medications even took them. "Amazingly, in America, even people who pay for medications didn't take them correctly at least 50% of the time. Third-party payers are trying to figure out a way to stop paying for medications that people don't take. I also had a life changing experience this... "

He was interrupted by a chime from the kitchen. Something there was ready. As they moved into the galley Sally was a little surprised that the table was set, there were candles ready to light and some fantastic aroma emanated from the stove. The good china was out, the cloth napkins were in place and the shiny silverware was on the table. As she looked at the stove she realized that Jack had gone all out for this meal. There was soup simmering in a pan. By the smell of it, she guessed it was Manhattan chowder, not New England chowder! Having grown up in the Midwest she was always surprised that Jack served red Manhattan clam chowder in Rhode Island and not white New England clam chowder. Jack had once explained to her that while he was growing up, he always had red chowder and was shocked to find out at a restaurant in Boston that New England chowder was white. Opening the stove, Sally immediately recognized the casserole dish with coquille Saint Jacques bubbling. She knew there would be chunks of linguica in there. On the top shelf was the flat pan with a layer of roasted potatoes, covered with rosemary and thyme and sprinkled with Portuguese olive oil. As Jack ladled out the soup, Sally put the pans on the stovetop to cool. They ate their soup in silence and then each helped themselves to the scallops and potatoes.

They both ate like famished children. Jack was overwhelmingly grateful for having someone to share dinner with. He had been thinking that Sally was quieter than usual and was surprised to hear her ask, "What's bothering you? You have very been quiet. You were about to say something before dinner. Have you been a bad boy again?" His raised eyebrow was answered with, "While the drinks and the meal have been wonderful, you did not check my back for a bra strap and did not pop it open with one hand like you usually do."

"With the sun shining through your dress, I didn't think you were wearing one," Jack offered weakly. He took her hand.

Usually, within minutes of meeting each other, they were tearing each other's clothes off so fast that they hardly made it into the cabin before they were both naked. Neither of them was loudly vocal during these encounters, considering how close the neighboring boats were, but they each thoroughly enjoyed these encounters. After so many years, they both remained inventive and attentive in their approaches to each other. Jack had come to realize that only complete surrender to your partner allowed these encounters to be fresh for years. Sally had been his teacher in this regard and he had finally become the excellent student he had been in all his other ventures. For too many years he had mistaken his undeniable attractiveness to women to mean he did not have to perform too. He had finally realized the burden of very attractive women; too much attention was not always a bonus.

On most Friday nights they were driving to find a bar or restaurant opened late at night in South County, Rhode Island for dinner. It was not as easy a job as you might imagine. That was especially true when the tourist season ended after Labor Day. Tonight they had sated their appetites first.

Jack took Sally's hand and led her to the bunk. They were both eager but they would take their time. Sally knew that eventually Jack would open up, but that would not be for the next couple of hours if not before morning. Considering her expectations right now, that conversation could wait till tomorrow. Sally was soon naked and lying on her stomach. Minutes went by, heightening her expectations. Jack was inspecting her with his eyes, was enjoying the inspection. "Jack, have you been a very bad boy this week?" she asked him again, in a whisper this time. More silence followed. She felt his lips on the back of her left knee. She felt a single finger pad on the inside of her left thigh, sliding upward. Her body shuddered. Tomorrow would definitely be soon enough…

Chapter 13

S HEILA PULLED HER UNMARKED squad car into the
visitor's parking of the administration building at 100 Ochre
Point Ave. Since this was a college rooted in the Catholic tradition,
she felt a little out of place. She did not feel threatened, however.
She was sure that she could get her job done during this visit. She
considered the elegance of the buildings that surrounded her. She
walked into the central hall and stood for a second, stunned at its
elegance. She knew that the original college had been started by
the Sisters of Mercy. In her background investigation, she had
not expected that group to be associated with the elegance of
this building. Her background research had revealed the college
had become a university in the '90s. She made her way to the
registrar's office, flashed her badge, introduced herself and asked
to speak to the registrar. The secretary picked up the phone,
spoke for a few minutes and waved her to the registrar's door.
Sheila knocked and entered after the response from within. Ruth
Barnes rose from her desk, shook Sheila's hand and invited her
to sit.

"How can I be of assistance?" asked Ruth after they were both
seated.

"I am here on a sensitive matter, looking for information," said
Sheila. "I am sure you have heard of the baby recently discovered

in a house on Thames Street. Our investigation has led us to believe that a student who was attending Salve Regina College in the late '80s might be connected to the case." As she outlined the story, Sheila watched Ruth's demeanor change slowly to one of grave concern.

"I am not even sure where to begin," said Ruth. "I'm not sure I can give you access to all our records from students that attended here at that time. It sounds like you are looking for a young lady who may have killed her baby while she was a student at this college! I am sure you can understand I cannot give you carte blanche to investigate student records. It seems to me you would need a subpoena of some kind, although as you describe the connection, we don't even know the name of the student we are looking for."

"I certainly understand your concern," said Sheila. "I am not sure we want to look at student records at this time. We were more interested in information about students that may have had a pregnancy, academic difficulties, social problems, or left school in the middle of the year. I would propose to start by having some discreet conversations with university employees who may have been here at the time it was still a college. If that did not work, we might want to expand to RA's that were working in the dormitories at that time."

"Oh dear," cried Ruth. "I am gravely concerned for the reputation of this university. You propose to have discreet conversations, but in a community as small as this, I can assure you that just waving your badge around is not at all discreet. Within minutes of starting a conversation with any of our employees, I would expect it to be all over campus."

"I am certainly open to any suggestions you or any of the universities' administrators might have. Surely you understand that since this is a potential murder investigation, we are not going to stop investigating just because someone or something might be inconvenienced. On the other hand we certainly do not want to do anything that will unnecessarily impugn the reputation of this university."

"Oh dear," repeated Ruth. "I am not sure how to proceed from here. I think I will have to discuss this with Sr. Jeanne Tremblay, the president of the university. I suspect she will consult with our attorneys or even the Board members. If you leave me your card I'll get back to you as soon as I have a chance to talk to her."

"You can't possibly expect me to leave this open ended. My boss won't be very happy that we're going to wait for a phone call from you. So far, the press has gotten no information to suggest that this university is involved in this case at all. That kind of information will get out sooner or later, and I'm sure you want to be ahead of that. On the other hand, there are several reasons we do not want to involve the press at this time. We are afraid that if they get wind of this connection, the person or persons involved might be frightened off and not cooperate at all. Of course if we get no cooperation from you here at the university, we may have to use the press to inquire whether anyone involved in the college at the time of this case could come forward with information."

"I see," said Ruth. "Excuse me for a minute while I go out to make a phone call."

Sheila sat quietly in her chair waiting for Ruth to return. It was longer than she expected but when Ruth returned she had someone with her. The newcomer was dressed in a nun's habit, was a little portly, looked like she could be quite stern but she had a smile on her face.

"Detective Goldstein," said Ruth, "this is Sr. Jeanne Tremblay. I think I will leave you alone at this point."

"No," said Sr. Jeanne. "I want you to stay to hear this conversation." She sat in Ruth's chair and Ruth sat in the chair next to Sheila.

"Good morning sister," said Sheila. "I am not sure how much Ruth told you about my reason for being here."

"I think I have the gist of the story," said Sr. Jeanne. "It is very distressing to think that anyone associated with this university would have anything to do with this kind of a matter. We would certainly like to help you in any way we possibly can, but some of the information you request may have to go through our attorneys to see what we can and cannot release. I understand that you can return with a subpoena, but I'm not sure what you would ask for if we don't know the name of the person we are what looking for. What exactly are you looking for us to do for you at this time?"

"I think initially we would like to be able to speak to several of your employees who may have been at the college at the time this incident occurred. We are looking for a student or students who may have behaved in an unusual manner. This young lady would have had to miss at least one week of classes during her ordeal in Providence. Maybe someone who'd been an excellent student had her grades fall off for a short time after this episode. Perhaps someone left the college unexpectedly or did not return for the next semester."

"I was actually teaching at the college at that time," said Sr. Jeanne. "I was a history teacher and virtually all students at one point or another came through my class. There are several other professors here who were also here at that time. I can have some discreet conversation with them to see if we can come up with some common names that would fill your criteria."

"It might also helpful if you have any janitorial staff still present," said Sheila. "They might remember an unusual event in one of the dorms where bed clothing or towels were discarded or more blood than usual was found in one of the dorms. Any security people from that time might remember unusual student activity in the middle of the night or a car parked out of place that might lead us in the right direction."

"Do you have a name as a starting point?" asked Sr. Jeanne.

"The name we have is Mary Murphy, but as I told Ruth, other information suggested that this was not her actual name. Her age suggested she would have been a freshman or sophomore in school at that time."

"A birthday or dorm room number or home address or phone number might be helpful," said Sr. Jeanne. "She may have used a made-up name but perhaps something about the rest of the information she gave she gave you would ring true."

"That's a great idea," said Sheila. "I'm a little embarrassed that I didn't think of that since I am supposed to be the detective."

"I applaud your candor young lady. I think you will find that as a former professor and now the president of the university, I have to use some detective skills more often than you would expect. Please give me one or two days and I will get you as much information as I can."

"Thank you very much sister," said Sheila. "I will see what other information I can get and forward it on to you. I will be sure to get it either directly to you or to Ruth so that no one else is aware of the investigation at this time."

Chapter 14

SALLY SAT NEXT TO THE front railing, waiting for instructions from Jack about what to do next. They were making their way into Narragansett Bay, just past Point Judith. She loved to sail with Jack as he was all business. He exuded confidence in his sailing ability. He carefully studied the wind, wave and tide patterns. Jack sat with his hand quietly on the wheel of his boat as they rounded the Point Judith.

After they had shared a great breakfast, he had slowly told her the story. She had expected some lurid confession and in a way that is what she had gotten. "Twenty years ago, I called the police on one of my patients. I took care of patient transferred from Newport Hospital who had obviously just delivered a baby. Problem was that she refused to acknowledge she had ever been pregnant!"

Sally's eyes had widened more and more as the details emerged. "How come I have never heard any part of this story before?" she asked incredulously. "I know you don't tell me about every patient but this was a particularly unusual story because of the obvious effect it had on you. I know it happened before we met, but still. It sounds like the parts about the police officers and the child protective worker that did nothing about your concerns are still very emotional for you."

Jack filled her in on the current questions from the Newport police and Sally agreed with him that it was not over. "I am worried about the can of worms that is being opened and I am not happy to be dragging you into it."

"Don't be silly. I want to know and I am grateful to be able to support you."

His attention turned back to sailing. He calculated that he needed to make two or three more tacks before they could set the spinnaker and fly north. Years before, he had deliberately docked his boat south of the bay. He knew it was too easy to sail from Barrington or even Newport. The summer wind virtually always blew from the South. It was easier to plan a day sail from the north; you could work your way down the bay as long as you liked and then you could turn north, set the spinnaker and fly home. From his berth at Snug Harbor, he could fly into the bay but coming home was the challenge. He was like the champion golfer who always played each course, no matter how hard, from the tips. Jack was proud of his sailing prowess and also proud that he didn't have to flaunt it to anyone else. He was the only judge of his ability and only people like Sally were even mildly aware of it. Of course Jack Junior was also aware of his dad's sailing ability. They had bonded together that summer long ago when they brought the West Sail through the Panama Canal to get to the East Coast.

Jack remembered the first time he had seen "The Stork". It was the summer of '75 and "Uncle Abe" had taken him out on it from Marina Del Ray. "Uncle Abe" was somehow related to his first wife but the connection had been vague. Jack had been terrified within 30 minutes of starting to sail with Abe as they tacked their way out the breakwater of Marina Del Ray. Jack was acutely aware that if he missed any signals from Abe they might end up on the rocks. Even after Jack and his first wife had broken up, Jack kept in touch with Abe and had flown out once or twice a year for sailing lessons. Abe had taught him sailing and navigation just as he had taught others at the Coast Guard Academy during World War II. From his wheel, Abe would get on the bullhorn and talk to nearby sailors, instructing them to tighten the jib or reef in the mainsail. Abe chuckled as they waved back, having accelerated by two or 3 knots over their previous speed.

Abe and Jack had sailed in all kinds of weather because Jack wanted to perfect his sailing technique as he had tried to perfect everything else he did. When Abe had told him that he had decided to sell the boat, they quickly negotiated a fair price and the deal was made. Abe had reassured Jack that he now had the sailing capabilities to take the boat through the Panama Canal and around Florida, up the East Coast and back to Rhode Island. Jack knew that Abe was happy to keep the boat in the "family" and Jack knew it was in tip top shape. It had a two year old Perkins diesel engine and 1100 ft.[2] of the best sails available. Abe had changed each winch and pulley as needed. Jack had taken Jack Junior on some of these trips but never expected to have him as a mate in the long journey to the East Coast. Still things had fallen in place for both of them.

In June of 1988, at age 19, Jack Junior had finally graduated from high school. Jack's ex-wife number two was also gone by this time. Jack knew that both of his marriages had failed because of him, but the second one failed with a big push by Jack Junior's wayward ways. The juvenile delinquencies had taken their toll and Jack wanted to find a way to reconnect with his son. College applications were still far off for Jack Junior because of his spotty school record and Jack knew by now that Brown University was out of the question for him.

"Dad, I want to sail the canal with you!" Jack Junior and insisted.

"Are you sure? It will be a long trip. There is no turning back. If you abandon me, I will not be able to finish alone."

"Dad, I know I have not always been reliable but I promise you I want to do this and I will stick it out to the end."

"I believe you! You have never seemed very keen about sailing but I would love to have you with me." For two weeks they had planned; Jack Junior had said repeatedly that he understood the commitment that would be needed for this trip. Jack had not needed to hire a second mate to accompany him. Finally, they had booked the airline trip to LA.

They had sailed for two 1/2 months. Jack felt guilty whenever they used the diesel; Abe would have been terribly disappointed. As expected, he and Jack Junior became completely reliant on each other. They literally had each other's lives in each other's hands. Jack had been skeptical at first but the team had worked well. They each had duties and carried them out. By the time they had passed Montauk Point, Jack was proud of Jack Junior and Jack Junior knew it. Jack had lost two wives, but finally had a family again, him and his son.

Chapter 15

Sr. Jeanne called Sheila two days after their first meeting.

"I have three possible names for you," said Sr. Jeanne.

"Great," said Sheila.

"First, Mary Jones. She was a freshman who started in September of '85. She was a local girl, a great student who started out strong but got into drinking and missed the first two weeks of the second semester. Then she reversed her activities and did well again until graduation. No one was aware of a pregnancy, but from what you told me she would have had to been pregnant before the school year started."

"I didn't think of that," said Sheila. "I'm surprised you did!"

"Even though I am a nun, I do know about how long pregnancies last!" said Sr. Jeanne. "She had a pretty good support system that several faculty members remembered. She was never trouble again and she has remained in the Newport community. She actively participates in alumni events. It would be a real shame if she was involved."

"The second candidate is Miriam Cohen," said Sr. Jeanne.

"Miriam Cohen?" asked Sheila. "I didn't know you admitted Jewish students here."

"We never have many, but even in the beginning, when we

were an all female college, we always admitted young women of any faith. Most often it was them who didn't want us. I think we were ahead of the curve in multiculturalism, in the present day vernacular. In any case, Miriam came to us in 1984 and would have been a sophomore in January of 1986. She was as sharp as a tack, vivacious and had a great personality. She had many friends right from the beginning. I remember her in class, she was engaging, showed good thinking processes, listened well to others' thoughts and ideas, and was never too pushy."

"So she seemed to fill in well here," commented Sheila.

"I didn't say that but now that you mention it, I think she was trying hard to fit in, especially at first. Rumor was that her parents were not too happy she came here. Still, her grades were great in her first two semesters. Her grades in the third trimester slipped a little. Over sophomore Christmas break, something happened because she was 2 to 3 days late starting the second semester. She didn't seem to have the spunk she had had earlier. She looked thin, almost frail as I remember. Everyone thought she'd had a row with her family. By the end of the semester she was back up to her old self or at least that is what we all thought."

"What do you mean?" asked Sheila.

"Well, three months before graduation she committed suicide by jumping off the Jamestown Bridge at three o'clock in the morning."

"Oh my God!" said Sheila. "What happened?"

"We are still not sure," said Sr. Jeanne. "She left no note. Her car was found still running, driver's door opened and front fender against the rail of the bridge. There were some suspicious skid marks near her vehicle but no contact damage was noted. Police thought that someone swerved to avoid her car. No one ever came forward even though it was front page news for days. Her body was never found, so that set off the press people even more. We had a long investigation here at the college, trying to decide if we had been supportive enough for her. Her family was great, worked with us and never pointed a finger at us. They had lost a daughter but they could see we had lost a child also. She received a diploma posthumously because she had done enough work even before her death to qualify for graduation. They knew she had been happy here and they still donate to our alumni fund. "

"I am speechless right now. I have a lot of questions sister, but none right now," said Sheila. "You said there was a third possibility?"

"The third name is Jean Wainwright," said Sr. Jeanne. "She was also a sophomore in '85/'86. She had had a child as a freshman, right after Thanksgiving. We almost did not let her start but she convinced us that she was committed to her pregnancy and her school work. She had a private adoption planned. We were impressed because she could have had an abortion but decided to keep her pregnancy and give the baby up. She gave us the name of her lawyer and let us speak to him. He was sure that she had her head on straight and we decided to let her continue with us. She worked hard and scraped her way to graduation after five years here. She was never a sterling student and had a few security breaches, you know, boys in the room past curfew. She never quite broke the party girl mold. She missed more than a few classes but no one remembers any special problems in early '86. She had a strong cadre of friends; all were well known to both security and administration. They all eventually graduated, thick as thieves, but in a good way."

"Interesting observation, sister," said Sheila.

"We had been coed for over 10 years by that time." said Sr. Jeanne. "Most of the faculty members before then were religious teachers, nuns and priests. Most were never fully on board with the mores of our young students. We had started to add more lay faculty members and after that we all got better at understanding the young men and women that we were serving here at our college. For a while thereafter, the boys stuck together like newcomers and the girls supported each other maybe even better than we did."

"Sister, you have been a great help! We will start crosschecking birthdays, old addresses, old family names, Social Security numbers, etc. As you reminded me, it is hard to make up a whole new identity without repeating part of a birthday or part of a name. If we get a solid lead on one of these girls, I will get back to you about some of the friends they had while they were here."

"You're welcome," said Sr. Jeanne. "I still hope this had nothing to do with Salve Regina. I still have a few maintenance and security people to talk to, but it will be harder to maintain discretion when I speak with them. If we can get it cleared with this information, I won't go there at all."

"I understand and thank you again," said Sheila. "One more thing, do you have some pictures of each student we can use to show the doctor to see if he recognizes any of them?" Sr. Jeanne nodded to Ruth and Ruth wrote it down. Sheila left with a boatload of checking to do!

Chapter 16

SALLY SAT NEAR THE BOW of the boat as they cruised up Narragansett Bay with the spinnaker flying. This was her favorite part of the sail; she had no special duties so she could spend some quiet time by herself. She usually settled on deck in a deck chair with a good book to read. She sat in her bikini catching some rays.

"Hey Sally, how about taking your top off? You know that I think that tanned breasts are the sexiest thing in the world." He chuckled as he waited for her response. He was amazed at how you could have a quiet conversation with someone at the far end of the boat when flying the spinnaker. It always seemed dead calm as the boat basically moved at the speed of the wind.

"Not going to happen," laughed Sally as she waved him off with her hand. She continued to resist Jack's hints about being topless. She had never felt comfortable being topless even when they are were in some remote destination. Certainly not the middle of Narragansett Bay. Still, she had made sure that all the appropriate tags on the suit were folded in place. She agreed with Jack that women who had $200 manicures, $100 pedicures, and a $400 bathing suits completely wasted their look when they had a tag sticking out. She found some of Jack's pet peeves quite amusing. "You'd think gynecologist would get enough of that at work."

"Never," said Jack. "You know why a gynecologist wears gloves at work, don't you?"

"Yeah, I know. It's so when he doesn't wear them he knows he's having fun." The jokes could never end thought Sally. Still, dating a gynecologist did have its positive points. If nothing else, you never had to slow down or stop to explain about the clitoris or the G spot. She had learned long ago that Jack needed no tutoring in those special places. Still, it'd taken her to teach him that being in total control was not always the best policy. Sometimes complete submission to your partner produced better results than you could ever have dreamed of.

She glanced back at Jack. He was still totally engrossed in his sailing. He checked the shore, he checked the wind, he checked the waves, he checked other boats, and he checked his compass. At this point she could just sit back and enjoy herself as he needed little help at this time of the trip.

As usual, Jack had planned the sail out very carefully. After checking the day's weather report, he had gone to his navigational charts to plot a course up the west side of Narragansett Bay into Wickford Harbor. He and Sally would then stop and have lunch and shop along the main street of town. He had nothing special he wanted or needed but he marveled at Sally's ability to be enthralled with the new line of clothing or canvases from local artists that would be available in town. He had never felt comfortable shopping with his wives, but he knew his presence was very much appreciated by Sally.

Despite the fact he seemed totally engrossed in his sailing, he often glanced in her direction on the bow. He totally respected her ability to be completely uninhibited and yet resist his urges to go topless on the boat. He remembered the day he unwisely reminded her that he often had other guests on his boat that could not resist his pleas to disrobe. She had so severely chastised him that day that he decided he would never go there again. They had a reasonably open relationship, but that did not mean she appreciated being reminded of it. He had often wondered if she had someone special that she saw in Vermont, but he was not curious enough to ask her about that. Actually, he was very curious about it. But they did not go down that road anymore. He knew that his unwillingness to move to Vermont allowed for her freedom there, just like her unwillingness to move to Rhode Island made her tolerate his activities while she was away. They were completely attentive to each other when they were together and that was enough.

Jack once again turned to sailing. As they neared the inlet to Wickford, he signaled Sally that they were ready to drop the spinnaker. Quarters here were very tight and it was one of the few places on the sail that he would start the engine to guide them into a public dock in Wickford. Once there, they spent a few minutes securing the sails and tying the boat to the mooring. Then they went hand-in-hand along Main Street to find a place for lunch.

After lunch and shopping, they proceeded up the West passage over the north end of Conanicut Island, and then turned down the East passage. This was always the part of the trip he enjoyed the most as it entailed tacking into what was normally a headwind and also working his way down the busiest part of Narragansett Bay. He expected to make Newport by late afternoon and had called the Newport Yacht Club to secure a mooring for the night. From the club, they could walk into downtown Newport. Even he enjoyed the kind of shopping that was available in Newport on Bowens and Banisters Wharfs. They could peruse the latest outrageously priced men's and women's fashions from New York or Europe. There were other stores to cruise, shoe stores, sunglass stores, sensible sailing jacket stores and galleries galore. From there they usually preceded to the Red Parrot on the corner of America's Cup Boulevard and Thames Street to have a dinner of seafood and beer. How nice it was to be able to return to the yacht club and have one of its workers row them back out to his boat at anchor so he didn't have to worry about his alcohol intake. He had been a longtime member of the club and Jack Junior had even worked there as a teenager, cleaning boats and ferrying customers back and forth to their boats. They would spend the night on board in Newport Harbor and then continue sailing back to Snug Harbor through the Galilee breakwater.

Jack's thoughts slipped to his latest trip into Newport. It was ironic that the baby that he had never found so long ago had turned up only a few blocks from where he often dined. He suspected he'd walked past that house 100 times during his trips into Newport. He wondered whether the police would ever find out exactly what had happened to the baby. He wondered if they would ever be able to identify the patient he'd taken care of so long ago. Their determination at this time contrasted starkly with the relative indifference that he had encountered in his original contacts with the police.

Chapter 17

LEAD DETECTIVE TONY FUENTES entered the conference room with Phil Hudson and Sheila Goldstein already huddled at the table. It was Labor Day and he was holding onto his sixth cup of coffee. He smelled of tobacco smoke.

"Okay, let's see where we are," said Tony as he sat down.

"We finally got some DNA evidence back," said Phil, "the lab was able to isolate a sample and we actually got a hit from CODIS. There is a 95% likelihood that this baby's father is Joaquim Del Rio, Jr."

"Shit!" said Tony. "Do not tell me that this is the son of Dr. Jack Dell Rio," said Tony, shaking his finger at Phil.

There was dead silence in the conference room as Phil and Sheila squirmed in their chairs.

"God dammit!" said Tony. "I knew this case was going to be a problem but you never know where the problem is going to come from. This is unbelievable. Why don't we start with why the hell this kid was in CODIS is to start with?"

"Well," Phil said starting slowly, hoping not to agitate Tony even more. "Evidently Jack Junior was not an altar boy when he was a teenager. He has quite a juvee record including some drug possession busts, a drunken driving accident, and a 14 month stint in jail. The jail time occurred because of an incident when he was 17 years old. At Halloween of 1985, he and a bunch of guys and girls broke into an abandoned home and had a drinking and sex party. They were mostly 15 years old and at the end of the partying, the house caught fire. The record is not clear on exactly who started the fire but only Jack Jr. was old enough to be charged with the violation. Despite his dad's efforts, and because of his previous violations, it did not go well. Even with the most expensive defense attorney in Rhode Island, he was convicted of participating in the event that got the fire started. Although he could have gotten 2 to 3 years on the arson charge, he was sentenced to 18 months and he served 14 and was let out on parole for good behavior. This Halloween incident also precipitated a statutory rape charge when one of the 15-year-old girls decided the next day that she had been coerced into having sex. Or her father decided there was no way she could have consented. Her father aggressively pushed the issue with the DA and one of the other boys was initially convicted of that charge. There was some confusion about the statute because both kids were only 15 years old. In the original interviews both the girl and Jack Junior testified that they had not had relations with each other. Towards the end of Jack Junior's sentence, the attorney of the young man originally charged with the crime produced DNA evidence that proved he had not been sexually active with the girl. The father then insisted the case be reopened and that's when Jack Junior submitted a DNA sample that also proved that he had not had sex with the girl. So that's why Jack Junior had a sample in the CODIS database, actually one of the first samples ever obtained in the late 80's for DNA verification."

"You guys know I don't believe in coincidences," said Tony. "Please tell me that this is not the girl who is suspected to be the mother of this baby."

"She's definitely not the mother of this baby," said Sheila. "First of all she is too young to have been in college and she would have been six months pregnant at Halloween to give birth to the baby 3 months later.

"I have been looking into the three names that Sr. Jeanne gave me, and none of them seem promising at this time. It sounds like we're going to have to go to the backup plan of talking to security people and maintenance people at the college when this incident occurred to see if we can get more leads. This is certainly going to make it easier for the direction of this investigation to become public because so far we have kept Salve Regina out of the press."

"I don't care what it takes," said Tony. "People, we have to find out who this baby's mother was. We cannot go forward with information about this baby's father when his father is the doctor associated with the case. He is someone who will bring down heavy legal representation for his son. We are going to need an open and shut case to get anywhere. For now we're going to keep quiet about the doctor's son's involvement in this case. I want no leaks about this: everybody on board?"

"Absolutely," chimed in Phil and Sheila together.

"Sheila, before we give up on them, please tell us the details of what you've gotten on the investigation of the three names that Sr. Jeanne gave you that make you feel we need more suspects. We may end up with the Salve Regina connection being a "red herring.""

"Well," said Sheila, "the preliminary investigations I have done so far aren't terribly revealing. I don't have any information that suggested that any of those three girls were pregnant in the first semester of the '85-'86 school year. They all had a shaky start that semester but Mary Jones, the first girl, was a freshman and that's not unexpected. Her academic record improved starting with her sophomore year.

"The second girl, Miriam, is actually related to a family I know from synagogue. Of course everyone there knows the family and knows about the tragedy of Miriam's death. Some very discreet questioning on my part reveals that no one remembers Miriam ever having had a boyfriend, let alone a pregnancy. I don't think we have a solid enough lead on any of these women to ask them or in Miriam's case, her family, for DNA samples.

"The third girl, Jean Wainwright did have a baby when she was a freshman, but there was no evidence that she had a pregnancy during her second year. It would seem strange that she would have been as forward with the school as a freshman and would have completely hidden a pregnancy as a sophomore.

"I am going to definitely look into the attorney that Jean Wainwright used for her private adoption in her pregnancy the year before. If that attorney is not someone who can contribute to this case, he may know of other attorneys in Rhode Island that were active in private adoptions at that time."

"Okay," said Tony. "I like that direction of inquiry. There must be someone involved beside the girl because she was probably hospitalized when the baby died. I would still like to look into the disappearance of Miriam two years later. Phil, I want you to look into seeing if we have any tire impressions of the skid marks that were found near her car and go over the forensic evidence that was obtained from her car on that night."

"Will do, boss," said Phil. "One more thing, Mr. Arnold called to say he had asked his wife about any unusual characters that might have rented the house on Thames Street and said she could not think of anyone. When I asked to speak to her directly, he told me she was not available."

"Well," said Tony, "keep looking for some connection between that house, any of the girls Sr. Jeanne mentioned and now Jack and/or Jack Jr. We need to start putting some things together or we are never going to get anywhere."

Chapter 18

JACK AND SALLY SAT on the deck of "The Stork" in Newport Harbor, having breakfast. They'd had a restful night. After dinner at the Red Parrot they had returned to the boat and had a nightcap. Their lovemaking on Saturday night had not reached the urgency of the previous night. Still, the slow lapping of the waves against the boat's hull, the sound of bells from buoys in the harbor, the sounds of motor boats, the sounds of traffic from the bridge, and even the occasional horn beeping added to the romance of being on board together. It had not hurt that there were several cries of passion from some of the surrounding boats at anchor.

After breakfast, Sally cleaned up from breakfast as Jack got the boat ready to sail. He first purged the bilge and then started the Perkins diesel. The congestion of boats at anchor and the traffic even early on Sunday morning produced too great a challenge to sail from their overnight mooring. They sailed south of Goat Island and only when Jack was due north of Fort Adams did he and Sally unfurl some sail. They sailed southwest past Beaver Tail light at the bottom of Jamestown, and passed Narragansett Beach and Scarborough Beach to the starboard side. After rounding Point Judith, they turned into the breakwater and approached the narrow causeway into the Salt Pond. As they approached the causeway, Jack dropped the sails and once again started the diesel to safely bring them him to his berth in Snug Harbor. After they had secured their lines, Jack went through his routine of securing the boat from its recent travel. Sally prepared some sandwiches for lunch and they once again sat on board to discuss their weekend.

The coming end of summer also meant that Sally would restart classes at Norwich Academy so on these Sundays she usually left in early afternoon to make her long trip back to Vermont. She could then spend some time in Vermont getting classes ready for Monday morning. Since Jack was planning to have dinner with his son and family, they hit the road at the same time. They followed Succotash Road to Route 1 N. and then continued on to Route 4 N. to its end where it dumped onto Interstate 95 north. 2 miles later they parted company as Sally went left onto Interstate 295 north, and Jack continued on Interstate 95 north to Cranston, Rhode Island. Jack was expecting that Sally would call him in about 3 to 3 1/2 hours to report that she had made it safely back to Norwich.

Jack turned off Interstate 95 in Cranston, Rhode Island and traveled several blocks to Jack Junior's house. They had set up a pretty comfortable routine in which Jack visited Jack Junior and his wife Donna on Sunday nights. They usually had dinner and perhaps watched a baseball game or a Sunday night football game. When Jack left Cranston on those Sunday nights, he continued north to his apartment in Providence to prepare for his two or three days of voluntary service at the free clinic in Providence. Jack no longer actively practiced in the hospital doing deliveries or surgeries. He still spent an occasional day with medical students. He had always been frugal with money, with only "The Stork" being an extravagant expense. Jack had won a large settlement and full custody of Jack Jr. after his divorce from wife number one, who just wanted to return to her high society friends. The settlement was substantial enough that he hadn't really had to work after that. He had later realized that her abandonment of him and Jack Junior had precipitated some of the events in Jack Junior's adolescence. He often wondered if his wayward ways had caused all the turbulence in Jack Jr.'s life but he had finally realized that the marriage had not been salvageable. Her flamboyant lifestyle and his long work hours could never have been reconciled. Although he could afford to retire early, he had felt selfish about not sharing his gifts and abilities in medicine. He had worked and studied hard to gain this level of expertise, so he had worked for 25 years in Ob-Gyn and now worked at the underserved clinic in a pro bono capacity

As Jack mounted the stairs on Jack Junior's porch, he once again marveled at how well Jack Junior, now aged 37, had overcome his previous travails. He had found Donna, settled down, and now they had two great kids. In the past 14 years Jack Junior and Donna had forged the kind of relationship that Jack envied. Their children, Mary age 8 and David age 6 were well-adjusted. They enjoyed hands on parenting from both Jack Junior and Donna. They both did well in school and enjoyed several sports including soccer and basketball. Jack Junior had settled down as an executive at a telecommunications company and Donna worked as an executive secretary in a legal office in Providence. Jack's proximity to them in Providence allowed him to occasionally meet one or both of them for lunch. They would meet at Joe's American Grill or the Cheesecake Factory at the Providence Place mall. Jack also liked these meetings because he could stop in the bookstore and look at the latest bestsellers. He particularly liked the medical mysteries of Michael Palmer and the Rizzoli and Isles detective series from Tess Garritson.

Chapter 19

SHEILA JOINED PHIL in his cubicle in the Newport police station. Phil had stopped to pick up some coffees and he was waiting for her at his desk.

"I think we need to compare our notes," said Phil. "I can see Tony getting really upset about this case and I'd like to make some headway before we meet with him again."

"I agree," said Sheila. "I am a little stymied on what direction to take next. I think we may be barking up the wrong tree with the names Sr. Jeanne gave us. I think I'm going to have to go back and see if we can get more leads there."

"I may be able to help with that," said Phil. "I spoke to the DNA specialist who's working with us on this case and he told me there were several markers in the baby's make up that strongly suggested it had some Jewish ancestry. For instance, it was positive for the Tay-Sachs gene."

"You're right," exclaimed Sheila. "That really narrows it down a lot. When I spoke to Sr. Jeanne, she told me that in any one year there were very few Jewish students who attended the college. This is either going to be a great game breaker, or else the Salve Regina connection will definitely be a "red herring"."

"When I heard that," said Phil, "I thought we should really consider investigating the girl, Miriam that you mentioned. I know this may be a little sensitive for you since you know the family from synagogue, but if this Jewish connection is really true, I think you're going to have to accept the fact that someone from the synagogue may be involved."

"I was afraid this might happen," said Sheila. "I have played it over and over in my head and I can't figure out how I'd approach Miriam's family for a DNA sample. Trying to introduce Miriam as a possible mother to the baby found on Thames Street presents a delicate situation. On the other hand, suggesting we need a sample to verify remains that have been recently found would be a lie and I don't think I could do that."

"Well," said Phil, "I could do that interview and request a sample if it seemed easier for you. Still, I would like your support if I ended up doing that. I have some other information that is very intriguing. I went back through the police reports on Miriam's car when it was found abandoned on the Jamestown Bridge. There were no obvious signs of foul play, but the investigating detective said he had never seen anyone simply walk away from a running car, leaving the door open, and jump off the rail of a bridge. You would expect there to have been a note somewhere, in the car or at her apartment. She had not done any of the things you usually see when a suicide is carefully planned; like paying off all her bills or cleaning and straightening her apartment. Her wallet, drivers license, and credit cards were all still in her wallet in her purse in the car. Interviews with her family had not suggested any depression or warning signs that she was contemplating suicide. It was as if, with no prior planning, she was driving over the bridge, decided to stop, jump out of the car and then jump off the bridge.

"The information on the skid marks by her car was also incomplete. It doesn't look like another vehicle crashed into her car or into the guard rail and there was no blood to suggest she'd been hit by a vehicle and thrown off the side of the bridge. The skid marks were behind her car so they did not think it had cut her off. There was only one unidentified print beside Miriam's and it was in a place that suggested the car had not been moved after Miriam left it. In the end, they had no reason to pursue it as a murder investigation.

"The skid marks were not identified at that time but when I showed pictures of them to one of our experts, he told me that the tires would have been on a very expensive vehicle, probably front-wheel-drive and the only ones that fit that description back then would be a Cadillac Eldorado, Oldsmobile Toronado or a Buick Riviera. Just for fun, I looked it up and Mrs. Del Rio number 2 was driving an '84 Buick Riviera at this time and it could have made those skid marks. I will investigate Jack Junior driving record a little further; maybe he borrowed his step-mom's car.

"It seems that in the summer of '85, when the pregnancy would have started, Jack Junior was working at the Newport Yacht club in Newport. Evidently his dad thought that having a job would keep him out of trouble for the summer, but it didn't work out as planned. It seems that Jack Junior had paid more than a professional interest in some of the yachtsman's daughters. He developed quite a reputation that summer that certainly did not help him with the Halloween incident in the fall. If we can put Miriam at the yacht club in the summer of '85 and Jack Junior on the Jamestown Bridge in January of '88, we would be getting somewhere."

Sheila had been quiet during Phil's monologue. He could see that her interest had been piqued during his discussion but his last statement had clearly left her skeptical. "I can see where you would be correct," said Sheila, "but 20 years later, we are going to have our work cut out for us if we are going to prove those facts.

I think we need to put a few more things together before we will convince Tony to bring Jack Junior in for questioning."

Although they both realized it, neither of them said anything about the fact that they were thinking of Jack Junior as a possible double murderer.

Chapter 20

DONNA ANSWERED THE doorbell, embraced Jack and gave him a kiss on the cheek.

"Hi, Dad, nice to see you again. How are you? How is Sally?" asked Donna.

"I'm good," Jack lied, "and Sally is great. I hope you got my message that she wasn't coming tonight because she has classes to prepare for school next week."

"I did, we'll miss her."

As he entered the hallway, Mary and David came bounding down the stairs to greet him. As Donna took his hat, the kids scurried off with him to the living room. They took turns telling him about their adventures for the week. There were soccer games to be summarized by both and an upcoming science project for Mary to outline. Jack listened attentively, surprised at the intensity of their descriptions. Their energy at this age amazed him and he wondered where he'd been for Jack Junior at this time of his life. It was no wonder that Jack Junior had rebelled.

Jack ruefully remembered that Jack Junior had often said, "Some doctors should not have children if they were just going to ignore them." Jack had resisted the temptation to complain he had expected some help, any help, from Jack Jr.'s mom. He'd always felt so guilty about his own behavior, he had never said anything.

Still, Jack had decided he was not going to make the same mistake with his grandchildren and he savored these nights as much as he would an excellent wine or single malt scotch. Perhaps, he considered, equating family tranquility with alcohol was a continuing problem for him.

Jack Junior had quietly eased into the room and was leaning against the door jam. He watched as his father and children interacted so easily with each other. In his childhood, he would never have dreamed this kind of domestic scene would occur in his house. His dad's patience with his children seemed effortless. Over the years Jack Junior had come to appreciate the accomplishments of his dad in his chosen profession. The 2 1/2 months at sea had strengthened their relationship. Certainly, Jack Junior could never establish any kind of relationship with his real mother who had walked out on both of their lives. Of course that non-relationship was probably better than the poisonous relationship he had had with his stepmother, but he knew that that was not all of his making. Jack Junior marveled at the relationship his father had with Sally. He knew that the two failed marriages had wounded his dad severely; dad had seldom failed at anything. He expected that dad would never settle down completely, but he was grateful for the stability Sally brought to his life.

Jack Junior's reverie was broken up by the dinner bell from the dining room. They all knew the price to pay for ignoring Donna's dinner bell, so they all dutifully marched into the dining room. Donna had become an excellent cook of Portuguese cuisine. They started off with caldo verde or green soup. Everyone searched around to see if the chunks present would be linguica or sal picau. Donna often alternated between the two and the first one to correctly identify the ingredient would have bragging rights for the rest of the week and no kitchen cleanup duty. David was the winner tonight! The soup was followed by a course of rib roast and roast potatoes, one of Jack's favorites. It was surprising how good Donna had become at these meals when neither of Jack's wives had ever mastered any kind of cooking. Happily, Donna's Italian heritage also made her excellent at that kind of cooking, and Jack felt himself doubly blessed in that regard. Portuguese or Italian cuisine, you couldn't go wrong!

"Dad," asked Jack Junior, "did David tell you he's scored four goals so far this season in soccer?"

"Well," said Jack, "we were getting to that but Mary was telling me about the science project she was doing on using solar cells to charge up batteries on an automatic alert system that would go off if a boat capsized. Sounds like I'm going to have to invest in one as soon as she gets it patented."

"Grandpa," said Mary, "you always exaggerate. First I have to win the science fair before I get it patented. I came in second last year but I'm not going to settle for anything but first place this year."

"Sure," said David, "my sports stories always take second seat while Ms. Chatterbox goes on and on about her science project."

"We are all ears, David," said Donna, "tell us all about those four goals that the Cranston JV midfielder scored against East Providence and Pawtucket."

Jack marveled that these dinner conversations were always about the children. Adult talk would come later.

When dinner ended, Jack Junior went upstairs with the children to finalize any homework they needed to do before the next week of school started. Jack helped Donna with dinner cleanup. Jack and Donna often swapped stories of their professional lives, doctors and lawyers having more in common than most people realized. When the baseball game started, Jack and Jack Junior would retire to the family room to watch, enjoying each other's company. They never rehashed the old days; conversation at this time always centered around current events and perhaps future plans for vacations. They sometimes went sailing for weekends and Donna and the children were becoming experienced sailors. As was their custom, Jack seldom spoke about medical matters, and Jack Junior's seldom spoke of his work. They had settled into a pretty comfortable routine and both were happy for that.

"Dad, I think it's time to get Mary and David started with skiing this year. Norwich Academy is reasonably close to several of the Vermont ski areas so we could rent a condo at Killington or Mount Snow and get the children enrolled in ski classes."

"That's a great idea," said Jack. "A recent study suggested that skiing was the best cross training sport for soccer players because they both require lots of leg and ankle rotation. Both children enjoy soccer and being outdoors so it seems like skiing would be a perfect fit. Since Sally would be close, this would be another way to firm up family gatherings through the winter, when summer activities like sailing fade away."

Jack Junior reminded his dad that Donna was not particularly fond of outdoor activity but Jack pointed out that most ski areas now had health spas where she could spend some time while they were out skiing with the kids. Jack was sure that Sally would sometimes go skiing with them and other times spend the day with Donna. Since Manchester was not that far away, the girls could also enjoy day trips for shopping. Jack Junior pulled out a calendar and they picked out a few weekend days that looked promising. They would each check their respective calendars and on the following Sunday, they would see if these dates would be a good fit. Around 10:30 PM, the game ended, Jack said goodnight to Jack Junior and Donna and headed for his apartment in Providence.

Jack parked in the garage of his apartment, two blocks from Rhode Island Hospital. He stepped through the door of his apartment and barely had time to drop his bags before he saw Suzie, the 22-year-old graduate nursing student who rented the back bedroom, approaching rapidly. She jumped into his arms, wrapped her thighs around his waist and kissed him full on the mouth. Jack groaned. Susie's social calendar must have been a bust this weekend. He was not going to get much rest on this night!

Chapter 21

PHIL HAD CALLED Tony and told him they had made some important discoveries but were in need of direction on where to go next. Phil and Sheila met Tony in his office around lunchtime and each brought a folder with them to review.

"What have you got for me?" asked Tony.

"I reviewed the DNA evidence with our expert," said Phil "and he seems to feel that this baby has some markers that suggest Jewish ancestry. You might remember that one of the names given to us by Sr. Jeanne was a girl named Miriam Cohen, and I know you don't believe in coincidences. Sheila knows the family from synagogue and it seems to us the next step would be to see if the baby is related to Miriam's mom or dad by getting a DNA sample. We have discussed several scenarios in which we would ask her family for DNA samples but neither Sheila nor I can come up with a reasonable explanation for the request. After all these years it would be terrible to involve her family if this case was not related to Miriam at all."

"I have thought about this a lot," said Sheila. "Even though I know this family, it's my job to make these kinds of inquiries. Phil offered to make the inquiries, but that's not fair to him or the family. I know I have to do it, I'm just not looking forward to it."

"Tell me what you know about the family," said Tony. "Is her mom or dad still alive, do they have any other children, and do you know if they ever talk about Miriam?"

"Both are very well known around synagogue," said Sheila. "They are very active in the community. They have a 35-year-old adopted daughter of Korean ancestry and no other children. She seems to be very active in the family business, and is very doting on her mother. It seems that Mrs. Cohen is a homemaker and she is very well liked by the other members of the Jewish community. The word is that Mrs. Cohen never got over Miriam's death and still doesn't believe it was a suicide. Sister Jeanne also told me that they still give donations to Salve Regina University in Miriam's name. I spoke to my mom about the family and it seems they do discuss Miriam and continue to be upset that her body has never been found."

"I have an idea," said Tony. "It was popular for a while when fingerprint and DNA evidence first became available that families would keep samples of their children's hair or fingerprints in case they went missing. Phil, look to see if perhaps we have samples of DNA from Miriam that we might be able to use to match to this baby."

"Great idea, boss," said Phil. "But DNA evidence was just starting to be used in the late 80s when Miriam died, so it's not likely we have a sample from her. Even if we had samples of her hair for instance, it took us a while to figure out we needed hair roots to do DNA testing"

"That's true," said Tony. "But let's check to see if her mom and dad gave samples to match to her body in case it was ever found."

"An even better idea, boss," said Phil, "that must be why they pay you the big bucks."

"Let's not get ahead of ourselves," said Tony. "Let's see what we got before we start congratulating ourselves. Now, I also understand we're trying to see if we can put Jack Junior on the Jamestown Bridge the night Miriam died. That's going to be a difficult job this long after death. It also implies we are considering that Jack Junior had something to do with both of these deaths."

"We also discussed that at great length," said Sheila. "This direction of investigation implies some sinister and dark motives in these cases. I think that even more than before, we have to be sure of where we're going before we start questioning Jack Junior. The most recent information we have on him is that he straightened his life out and it would be a shame to revisit those early delinquencies if he's not truly involved."

"Well," said Tony, "he is truly involved because the baby was his. If we can prove that the baby was Miriam's, that will prove that they got together. We won't have to put Miriam at the Newport Yacht Club because they could have gotten together anywhere. Why don't we start with something a little bit easier? I understand that Jack Junior had several traffic tickets for speeding and one for DUI. Let's see if any of those police reports put him in his stepmother's car. That would be another coincidence that would be convincing enough to bring him in for questioning. It's not a question of if we're going to talk to Jack Junior; it's only a question of when and under what circumstances. But let's remember that his dad paid for the best legal advice available in the past and I don't want to tip our hand too soon. "

"Phil is still working on talking to the Arnolds to see if we can see how that angle fits in with the rest of the case," said Sheila. "And I am still planning to go talk to the adoption attorney that Sr. Jeanne told me about. I've tentatively made an appointment to talk to him about private adoptions in general, but I think he will be sharp enough to relate my questions to this case. Some guidance by you on how aggressive I should be if he makes the connection would be helpful."

"That will be a tricky situation," said Tony. "I leave it to your discretion on how to proceed if he realizes what this is all about. Sooner or later the direction of our investigations is going to come to light. The longer we have control of the direction of questioning, the better I like it. For now, as long as there are no leaks to the press, I think we'll be okay. Most of the people we are talking to would not benefit by involving the press, and most of them would probably prefer the press not be involved. Good job people, the facts of this case maybe starting to come together. Actually, still as clear as mud."

As they broke up, Sheila was pleased to learn that Tony trusted her discretion. She liked that!

Chapter 22

JACK WOKE UP a little after 8 AM on Monday morning. One of the great advantages of being retired and a volunteer was that you didn't exactly have to be in on time every day. Still, he was due at the clinic at 9 AM and he would make that with no trouble. As he fully woke up, took in his surroundings and remembered where he was, he realized that Suzie was still spooning against his back. He rolled over. It was Suzie, just as he expected. She was naked, just as he expected. She was late for her morning shift, not what he expected. He knew that Suzie was a great worker at the hospital and it was only 10 minutes away, but she did have a habit of being late on occasion. The first time it happened she had horrified him by telling him her explanation to her supervisor: "the old guy I room with wanted sloppy seconds this morning!"

It took him a second to realize she had been kidding! This morning he gently woke her up and sent her into the shower. He ran into her room and gathered the things that she needed for work that day. Of course instead of standard bra and panties, he got her some frilly stuff that she usually didn't wear to work. Still, she had a newly laundered nursing outfit that had been starched and ironed by him last week. He went back into his bedroom, made the bed and laid her clothing out for her.

"Are you enjoying yourself, watching me dress in these

provocative under things?' she smirked. "Are they for the benefit of that intern I told you about or are they for you later?"

"Actually they are for me to remember all day today. And maybe there will be another intern story for you to tell me about later." She finished dressing, kissed him on the cheek, put her hands on her hips and wiggled them. She ran out the door and went to work.

Jack then showered and shaved to get ready for work at the clinic. He drove several blocks to the clinic and got there just after 9 AM. The waiting room was already full even though the first appointment of the day was at 9 AM. The director of the clinic was a former student of Jack's that had gone to medical school later in life after a successful career in the stock market. Since his financial goals had been met prior to graduation he had dedicated his life to the working poor and non-insured in Rhode Island. He had specialized in family practice and at every clinic session there were two or three third or fourth year medical students from the Brown University program working with him. He usually also had a family practice resident overseeing the students and of course, either he or Jack would then supervise the resident. Since Jack's specialty had been obstetrics and gynecology, he was often steered to those patients for help in that regard. Still, after a lifetime of obstetrics and gynecology, he had to relearn how to become good at listening to lungs and listening to hearts. Checking for kidney infections and evaluating belly exams reminded him of his residency or early practice days. Since gynecologists also spent a lot of time doing breast exams on their patients, Jack often offered counsel on those patients too. He was not a trained breast surgeon and he had never really done breast biopsies in his practice but he certainly had some experience in doing these exams and referring patients for mammography or to a breast surgeon for evaluation when needed.

Jack checked up on labs that he had ordered in the previous two weeks and then checked his e-mail to see if there were any messages he had to deal with at this time. The medical students sometimes came directly to him with simple evaluations but with more difficult evaluations, they had the resident see the patient and then the team would come to see him. Since Jack loved patient interaction, he often went into the room just to shake their hand and introduce himself. He would listen to the student or resident explain the treatment protocol they had decided upon. As the students grew in confidence, he would let them do the explanation, only correcting significant discrepancies in the plan. He found the family practice residents particularly interested in his opinion in gynecologic cases since most of their attendings were not completely comfortable with those kinds of cases.

The first patient they saw was a 37-year-old Medicaid patient who was there for her sixth pregnancy, approximately 8 weeks along at this visit. She was dismayed because after her last delivery she had intended to have a tubal sterilization but the Medicaid rules that required a 60 to 90 day waiting period did not allow her to have the procedure immediately after delivery. Unfortunately, she had been lost to follow-up. In Jack's experience, the typical result of these cases was another pregnancy. Originally, the 60 to 90 day waiting period had been instituted to prevent physicians from coercing patients into having sterilizations that they were not ready for. Since the patient had to sign and then re-sign the request for sterilization, it was felt that any coercive pressure could be obviated by the patient not showing up or not re-signing at a later date. It was a great theory that in practical terms meant that many of these women did not get appropriate sterilizations and ended up with two or three more unwanted children. As a new OB patient, she was the family practice resident's responsibility. Jack sat and listened carefully as he was presented the case. The third year medical student who had seen the patient with the family practice resident had added some important details to the patient's history. He was pleased to see that the resident had inquired if the patient wanted to continue the pregnancy, which she did. They ordered the appropriate prenatal lab work including HIV testing and offered to schedule the patient for a "quad screening" for trisomy 21 (Down Syndrome). Although they offered this kind of screening to everyone, since she was over age 35, an age designated as advanced maternal age, it was particularly important to document that she been offered the test. After listening to Jack's explanation of the test the first few times, most of the family practice residents had become very good at giving patients the information needed to making an informed decision. In this case, since all her other children had been normal and she felt that under no circumstances would she terminate the pregnancy, she decided not to have that test scheduled. They went on to explain to her that she could have most of her prenatal visits at the free clinic but sometime later on in the pregnancy, they would have her seen by the family practice residents at the hospital to prepare her for delivery. After the medical part of the visit, she was seen by social services to evaluate her for the WIC program that provided her with the dietary needs the growing pregnancy would demand. If any of the questions on the domestic violence screening panel had been positive, social services would also arrange to visit her home and check on the rest of her children. Jack had been amazed at how easily people adapted to these invasive questions and visits to secure medical care for their pregnancies. Certainly early access to medical care was one of the most critical determinants to a good pregnancy outcome.

The second patient Jack saw that day came in with a complaint of vaginal discharge. Her history was rather uncomplicated and he felt the acting intern (a fourth year medical student) who had evaluated her was ready to do a speculum exam on the patient. This particular student had traveled overseas with the family practice group and was adept at doing these types of exams. The initial evaluation suggested nothing more problematic than a yeast infection so they prescribe the appropriate medication for the patient and she left happy.

The third patient frightened Jack more than a little. She was an 11-year-old girl with very problematic asthma. She was on a long-term medication supplemented by daily inhalers. Despite these medications, she came to the clinic every other month with an acute exacerbation of her asthma. Jack understood that all the new medications available for asthma had made patients lives better, but there was also a rising concern at the number of young people who died despite aggressive treatment. No one was quite sure what was going on. There were some thoughts that these children had their asthma controlled so well by these new medications that when they became critically ill, they and their parents did not recognize exactly how sick they were. Certainly, having taken care of many high-risk obstetric patients, Jack had taken care of a lot of asthmatics during his career. Surprisingly, despite the extra demands on the pulmonary system associated by pregnancy, the high steroid levels often made these patients a little easier to control. Jack made sure the family practice resident had evaluated the patient's chart and discussed her case with her and her parents and after making some preliminary decisions on how to proceed with her care, Jack went to see the patient. He pulled out his stethoscope and made a show of examining her lung fields, front and back. He took a little time between listening front and back to let her catch her breath. He was concerned about some of the wheezes he heard in her lungs and realized that she was not under good control at this time. He saw the slightly bluish tinge in her lips and he looked at her fingernails to see if they seemed like they were being well oxygenated. He spoke directly to the little girl, seeing the fear in her eyes, while keeping an eye on her parents. He then discussed her case directly with her parents and he decided that the resident had evaluated the patient appropriately. He turned the rest of the discussion over to the family practice resident and they outlined the plan to admit her to the hospital for some aggressive treatment and to start antibiotics as they felt she had at least a mild infectious component to this asthma attack.

After this particular patient encounter Jack spent a few minutes with the family practice resident and the medical student that had seen the patient with him. He liked to point out that he almost always spoke to young people like they were his patient, as indeed they were. He did not ignore the parents and brought them into the conversation. If they answered all his questions directed to the patient, he would wave them off and tell them he would let them have their turn. He told the resident and student that they should always address the patient's concerns and either acknowledge them or explain why they were not pertinent in this case. Then you could go on and tell them about the discoveries you made during the exam that justified the treatment protocol you wanted to institute, especially if it differed from what they expected. That was the best way to make sure that everybody's concerns were met and no one felt left out.

Chapter 23

PHIL SAT WITH Harold Sturgis, the leading investigator of the Rhode Island's State Police DNA lab. The investigator looked like he was about 15 years old. After the first five minutes, Phil recognized that Harold was way smarter than he was. During that short time, Harold spoke three 30 word sentences that actually made sense. Of course on occasion he added in some technical language that Phil needed to have clarified and Harold was very adept at bringing the terminology down to Phil's level.

"We don't have any DNA evidence directly from Miriam," said Harold. "There was no struggle at the crime scene and since the thought was that it was a suicide, no effort was made to get the kind of samples of hair or a toothbrush that we commonly do now. Remember that this was the beginning of the use of DNA in crime labs. From what you have described to me, if two years earlier, at the baby's birth, some bloody bedding had been saved; we would now be able to try to match that to the baby. I understand that Sheila has not pursued talking to maintenance people but I doubt very much that we would have any ability to recover DNA from the dorm room even if they could identify which one it was.

"On the other hand we did better with the parents or at least with the mom. In 1994 she actually gave a sample of her blood for DNA analysis in case a body was found that needed to be identified as her daughter. The father did not participate in this sample collection and I understand he was not happy that his wife had participated. Accessing those old samples I can tell you that Mrs. Cohen is a 25% match to the baby which certainly suggests that she is a grandparent. If you get me a sample of Miriam's dad's DNA, I can just about verify for you that this baby belonged to Miriam."

"Well this certainly suggests that we are going to have to speak to Miriam's parents at some point," said Phil. "Tony, Sheila and I have all tried to think about how that interview would go. Her dad was reluctant in the past to give us a sample when we were trying to potentially identify her remains. There's no way to breach the subject with them without implying that Miriam may have had something to do with the baby's death. I'm not sure how we can convince them to give us a sample. What about the sample with Jack Junior? Have you been able to look that over and confirm for me that you think he is the baby's father?"

"Yes, I did look at those samples also," said Harold. "He had a very old sample on file and to the best of my ability, it certainly looks like he probably fathered the child."

"What are we talking about here?" Asked Phil. "We're talking 50%, 75%, 90%, what are we talking about?"

"I think we're talking about 95 to 96% likelihood that Jack Junior is the baby's father. If you give me another sample from Jack Junior, then I can firm up those percentages," said Harold.

"That's another sticky situation," said Phil. "We certainly have enough information already to probably warrant a court order to have him give us a DNA sample. We were hoping to have the first interview be pretty informal so if we rush in with a court order

I'm sure he's going to ask for a lawyer and we will be spinning our wheels for weeks."

"With my extensive experience in these matters," said Harold, "the 95 to 96% likelihood usually results in the person of interest giving you another sample without a court order."

As Phil looked at Harold, he wondered just exactly how much extensive experience he could have at his age. His expression had been noticed by Harold and Harold offered, "Yeah, I know you think I'm not much more than a schoolboy but I want you to know that I graduated with a PhD in this topic at age 20 and I have been working for the state police for the last eight years."

"I was not questioning your authority in these matters," said Phil. "I guess I really was wondering about your age but I was not going to ask you directly about that. I came for your opinion because I heard you were the best and the only question I have for you, is exactly how well you do in court when testifying?"

"I've testified in about 60 trials at this point," said Harold. "I can assure you that no defense attorney has bested me yet and that most of them don't even question my credentials anymore."

Chapter 24

ALTHOUGH THE CLINIC morning had been very hectic, Jack managed to sit down with Jonathan Krieger, the clinic director, for a short lunch. They were joined by the family practice resident, and the two medical students. Hero worship would be a good way to describe how the residents and medical students treated Jonathan. The selfless time he donated to the free clinic was legendary. He had won a few awards in his career and any monetary gains had always been turned back to the clinic. In the three years that Jack had been volunteering at the free clinic, this was probably only the fourth time that they had had enough time to sit down and chat at lunch. Jonathan was quiet and unassuming and a joy to talk to. He almost always managed to return the conversation to the students; their hopes and career goals. He was always encouraging to them and the walls of his office were papered by notes from earlier protégés he had directed. After this short break, they all went right back to seeing patients in the clinic.

The first patient of the afternoon that Jack was consulted on was a 37-year-old patient who was there because of infertility. Jack often considered how ironic it was that he would step from one room where a patient was going to terminate her pregnancy because it was not wanted only to find that the next patient was here with the heartbreaking story of her inability to achieve pregnancy. He often considered how great it would be to hook these families up so that one patient didn't have to terminate her pregnancy and could simply turn her baby over to the patient in the next room. It was only a pipe dream of course, because if nothing else, the latest HIPPA rules would never allow such a mingling of patient records. It would never work anyway, Jack thought. The patients that were unselfish enough to carry the pregnancy to term almost always decided to keep the baby. The infertility patient was so blinded by her desire to have a baby that they often missed telegraphed signals from the surrogate that they were not going to give the baby up at the end of the pregnancy. In any case, Jack listened to the history supplied to him by the medical student and they came up with a plan to do some simple tests to help decide what the infertility was about. Many of the tests for infertility were very expensive and even if the patient had some insurance, it usually did not pay for infertility workups. Accordingly, these procedures could not be fraudulently billed but an exam to look for active sperm after a recent sexual encounter could be coded as a test looking for cervical or vaginal infection. A saline infusion sonogram looking for polyps could often take the place of an x-ray dye test that was almost exclusively used for infertility evaluation. Jack was pleased to see that this student had been down this road on several other occasions and had picked up the lingo and expertise to start an appropriate evaluation and keep the costs reasonable. Jack had gone into the room for a handshake and also to reassure the patient they would do everything they could but also to warn her that these tests were not rapid. It might take many months for her to achieve her desired pregnancy, if ever.

The next several hours were filled with patient encounters

that would be similar to any family practitioner or emergency room physician. There were some scraped knees, sprained ankles, typical cold symptoms, and maybe even a flu patient. The flu would be unusual at this time of the year so the student had dutifully inquired about recent overseas travel by that patient. Jack was very pleased to see the interest and professionalism of the students flourish as they spent time in the clinic together.

The last patient of the day Jack saw with the family practice resident. The patient had recently given birth to her fourth child. The resident had actually done her delivery. Continuity care of patients was something Jack was concerned had been missing from medical school curricula and one of the best aspects of this free clinic was that they got to see the same patient over and over. In this case everyone had been pleased that her pregnancy had gone smoothly; she'd had her first girl after delivering three boys. She was currently 6 to 8 weeks after delivery and they had identified no problems from the pregnancy. Jack had often taught that the definition of a normal pregnancy was that patient, child and delivery had been completed six weeks ago and no one had identified any problems with any of the three. The patient had also complied with Jack's typical request that she bring the baby with her for her post partum checkup. He made a great show of unwrapping the baby to check its fingers and its toes and commenting on the color of her hair and that the baby's eyes had not fully changed color yet. Of course the students knew that his secret agenda in this exam was to see if the baby was being treated properly. A dirty diaper, a telling bruise or a twist of skin on the baby's arm or leg could be a sign of abuse. Unfortunately, he had occasionally been shocked by a cigarette burn and he taught the students that any sign of abuse required mandatory reporting to Child Protective Services. He often ruefully thought about his case from 20 years earlier; he had complied with the rules as they were laid out for him and other healthcare workers. There just seemed to be no consequences on the other side if they failed to follow up.

As the day was ending, Jack got a call from Jack Junior. This was not unusual as they occasionally made plans to get together after work or perhaps for Jack to sneak a quick trip down to visit the children. Jack was hardly ready for the information that Jack Junior had been requested by the Newport police to come in for an interview. Jack asked Jack Junior if he had been told what the interview would be about. The Newport police had not been forthcoming about the topic but had told him that it was only preliminary and they did not think he needed to bring an attorney with him. Of course, considering his past, this had rung several alarm bells in Jack Junior's head and that's why he had called his dad for advice. Jack inquired if Jack Junior was worried about anything that had transpired in Newport of late but Jack Junior could not come up with anything. Jack Junior asked if his dad would accompany him to the interview and although Jack had reservations about that, he said he would. Jack did not expect that they would let him sit in on even a preliminary interview. Still, he would go with Jack Junior for support and to remind Jack Junior that if any questions seemed strange, Jack Junior should not hesitate to request an attorney be present for any further questioning.

Chapter 25

SHEILA SAT QUIETLY in the waiting room of attorney Howard Baines. Mr. Baines had taking care of the private adoption that Jean Wainwright used for the baby she delivered as a freshman at Salve Regina College. Sheila had only gotten this interview by assuring the office that they would not be talking about Jean. She had decided that trying to interview Mr. Baines without mentioning Jean Wainwright would blow up in her face and she would get nowhere. Mr. Baines 'secretary escorted her into his office and quietly closed the door as she left.

Sheila introduced herself and showed Mr. Baines her badge.

"Would you outline exactly what brings you here, and then I can decide if we should proceed with this interview," said Mr. Baines.

"Mr. Baines, I am here to get some background information on private adoptions in Rhode Island around 20 years ago. It should come as no surprise to you that this is about the baby that was recently found on Thames Street here in Newport. Although one of your former clients, Jean Wainwright, was initially identified as a person of interest, I can assure you that she is no longer a suspect in this case. We are virtually certain that we have identified the mother of the baby that was found. Since there is great wonderment about what happened to the baby, one of the leads that we are pursuing is that perhaps the baby was initially given up for adoption."

"Howard, you can call me Howard, Sheila," said Mr. Baines. "As long as you assure me that we will not be looking into patient/ client confidentiality, I am happy to give you general information about private adoptions."

"Clearly you and your law firm handled some private adoptions around the time of this incident," said Sheila. "Assuming you were not involved in this case, I was wondering if you could give me some information on other law firms in Rhode Island, including some as far away as Providence that might have also done some work in this area. I'm sure that on occasion, a private adoption involves an attorney for the mother as well and as an attorney for the adoptive parents, so I assume you must have worked with other law firms in this area."

"Yes, you are correct," said Howard. "My office did work with several other offices in Rhode Island and also nearby Massachusetts and Connecticut. I took the liberty of having my secretary make a list of those firms that I could remember us working with 20 years ago. Some of the names should be very familiar to you because they represent very powerful law firms in Rhode Island. Some of them are still actively practicing, and some of the partners that handled adoptions back then have retired. Of course, I doubt that any of them would speak directly to you if the case involves one of their clients. You know as well as I do that that would involve client-attorney privilege."

"Hypothetically, what if the client we were discussing was no longer alive?" asked Sheila.

"Wow, that is a very big hypothetically," said Howard. "Hypothetically, what would have been the cause of death?"

Sheila took a deep breath and sighed. "The official cause

of death would have been suicide, but there is a scenario that involves homicide."

"Well," said Howard, "if it involves a suicide, I think most offices would consider that attorney-client privilege still holds. Of course, you know that if a felony was committed, since attorneys are "officers of the court", a subpoena might be successful in having some records turned over. I would think it would have to be a very specific request, not a fishing trip, and I would think the attorneys would not be currently employed by the potential suspect."

"If we got a subpoena for the victim's attorney, do you think we might be able to look at some records?" asked Sheila.

"If I understand your question correctly," said Howard, "I think most attorneys would make those records available."

"Thank you for your time, Howard," said Sheila. "You have been very helpful to me."

"Wait," said Howard, "can you tell me if you have a victim and if you identified the law firm that represented her?"

"No, I can't," said Sheila. "This is an open investigation; we are not sure where it's going to lead, and to be perfectly truthful, we are not sure her next of kin would know if she'd been using an attorney's office."

As she drove away from Mr. Baines office, Sheila could not know that Phil had not had a successful interview with the Arnolds. He had spoken to Mr. Arnold who had no new information for him and Mrs. Arnold was not available to speak to him, again. Although Mr. Arnold had been surprised to hear from Phil, he made no objections to talking to him without his attorney being present, and he had said he looked forward to hearing from Phil again if any further developments occurred in the case. Phil told Sheila for the second time that he thought this was a dead-end.

Chapter 26

JACK STOPPED AT THE local supermarket and picked up a few things before heading home to his apartment. Since Suzie was doing a double today, he was going to spend some quiet time alone at his apartment. Although he enjoyed his solitude, the one thing he did not like was eating alone. That had been his initial reason for renting out the back room of his apartment. Clearly he did not need the income. Some companionship was all he had ever expected but somehow he and almost each tenant had eventually become more intimate. It usually started with the massage table in the exercise room and progressed from there. He suspected his occasional solitary meals worked well for his weight control, because he seldom made an elaborate meal for himself. Tonight he made a small salad for his daily dose of roughage. He made a small hamburger patty from the 93% fat free ground beef he had picked up and he put this on a whole wheat bun. He sliced a tomato to garnish the hamburger and added some ketchup and mustard. Although he usually accompanied this meal with a handful of frozen French fries cooked under the broiler, tonight he added some chicken noodle soup. All of this preparation took him about 20 minutes and he finished eating in the next 10. Thirty minutes down and five and a half more hours to bedtime. Jack absentmindedly rode his exercise bike for 45 minutes while he glanced over the latest Green Journal of Obstetrics and Gynecology. Willie Nelson was playing on the stereo while he earmarked several articles he really wanted to sit down and review. He found that at this point in his career he was almost more interested in reading about topics outside of obstetrics and gynecology. He had become disillusioned reading about the latest developments in his own field because he felt many of the main topics were just being rehashed. In this late summer week, the Red Sox had Monday night off so he didn't have the option of watching the game. He did some laundry, even checking Suzie's hamper to see if she had things he could help her with. Just before bed he spent a few minutes contemplating his day at the clinic. As he reviewed his day, he fell back on his usual routine of thinking of five things he could have done better. Maybe he could have explained the difference between an IUD and the progesterone implant for contraception. Maybe he could have listened to the patient's complaint instead of taking over the conversation prematurely. A recent study showed that busy doctors listened to a patient for about three minutes before breaking into the conversation. He considered that this exercise of reviewing his performance at the end of each day was probably responsible for him having improved his skills as a physician. He also considered what his teaching role had been to see if he felt he was moving in the right direction with each of his resident and student colleagues. Like any good coach, he always tried to fit his teaching style to the capabilities of each learner. He also tried to fit his correction or discipline technique to their differing temperaments. He knew that some responded well to a firm correcting hand while others required praise and tolerated almost no criticism. He frequently reminded each of them that they could never evaluate how good they were, only others could do that. They, on the other hand, were the only ones who knew how bad they were. It was too easy to mess up, come out smelling like a rose and accept praise over what was actually a bad performance. They had to discipline themselves on these occasions to accept their near misses.

He woke up on Tuesday morning looking forward to another productive day in the clinic. His nagging doubts about the upcoming interview of Jack Junior by the Newport police had receded into the background. At this point he was fully confident that Jack Junior had done nothing to warrant any concern. He saw Suzie fleetingly in the kitchen as she ran out the door for her day's work. They often spent days just waving at each other as they went about their separate lives. Jack often wondered how the younger generation could be fully engaged at one minute and then totally disengaged the next. He suspected it had something to do with texting or video games that required intense concentration for short periods of time that was then followed by complete concentration in another topic altogether. He found it disconcerting that he could be standing in front of an information booth completely ignored by the person in front of him while they answered questions to some anonymous caller on the phone. He kept these complaints to himself as no one seemed to understand what he was talking about when he made them public.

Jack arrived at the clinic a few minutes after nine. The same family practice resident he had worked with on Monday was present for patient visits that day. On the other hand the student group was entirely different on Tuesday. Since it was late summer, the third-year students were undergoing the shocking transformation they all went through as they started gaining clinical expertise. The first two years of medical school were almost exactly the same as their highly advanced high school classes and their college classes. They were excellent students, which meant they had always been able to figure out what the teacher or professor wanted and they had been able to give them what they wanted. Jack always told them that coming into the third-year of medical school was a complete educational paradigm shift, the most difficult shift of their lives. They had left the world of academics. They would now be working with residents, physicians and patients, most of who had no idea what they wanted from the students. Most of their "teachers" had actually had no teaching instruction of any kind. They would find the first few rotations in the third-year very frustrating because their academic compass had been lost. They could be fully prepared for patient care that day and when they arrived at the clinic or on the patient floors they realized their resident was a having bad day and therefore they were going to have a bad day. Jack usually consoled them by pointing out that this would be exactly like taking care of patients for most of their professional lives. No matter how much they knew and how hard they worked, there would be days when nothing went right. They were not always convinced that this was consoling news. The great contrast was the fourth year medical student acting interns, who had taken a year to adapt to this new paradigm. Their growth in intelligence and capabilities and their people handling skills were markedly improved in just one year's time. Jack's direction with the fourth-year students was to make them as confident about their abilities as he could while still gently corrected any misstep they took. Jack always felt that training physicians was like bringing up your children. You had to let them make mistakes that could be corrected while not letting them make fatal mistakes or mistakes that were damaging to their patients. His success at these goals varied from day to day which is why he always spent time contemplating improvements he could have made before bedtime.

Chapter 27

Tony, Phil and Sheila sat in the coffee room. They were comparing notes so that they could interview Jack Junior.

"Okay, let's see what we got," said Tony.

"We now have some pretty good evidence from the DNA part of this investigation," said Phil. "I spoke at length to our DNA expert and he tells me that Jack Junior is the father of this child and it is very likely that Miriam is the mother of his child. I would suggest that we need to interview both Jack Junior and Miriam's family to see if we can figure out not who, but what was going on at the time this child was born. There is no circumstantial evidence of any kind that puts Jack Junior at his child's birth or demise. The circumstantial evidence also puts Miriam in the hospital with Dr. Jack at the time the baby died. Jack Junior will be coming to the precinct tomorrow for us to interview. I did not tip him off as to what we would be discussing but I did tell him he did not need an attorney for this interview, which is probably more than a little misleading."

"You know what I always say," said Tony. "When you talk to a suspect without an attorney around, their reactions to questions are probably more important than how they actually answer the questions. You certainly never get that openness when there is an attorney present jumping up and down and telling their clients to refuse to answer that question. On the other hand, interviewing a suspect with an attorney present is sometimes revealing when the attorney does object to a particular question. When they object and what they object to is often revealing about what they know about the case based on what their client has told them. These cat and mouse games often have two experts present, the plaintiff's attorney and hopefully us. Most of the time the suspect is not an expert at how these interrogations go but in the case of Jack Junior, we almost have to expect that he's an expert also since he's pretty smart and he's had a lot interactions with the police and attorneys in the past."

"What is your plan for interrogating Jack Junior?" asked Sheila.

"I think I'm just going to have Phil talk to him informally," said Tony. "I think I may just sit back as an observer and I'm going to use the interrogation overview room and take notes. I will jump in only if I feel like I really have to, because I think two of us questioning him would put him on extra alert."

"Where do you want me to start, boss," asked Phil. "I thought I'd be straightforward and ask him if he knows Miriam Cohen to see his reaction. If we get a reaction from him on that question I will continue pursuit of that angle. If not, I may ask him about the summer of '85 and his employment at the Newport Yacht Club."

"That may be the best way," said Tony. "Sooner or later the timeframe of what we're talking about is going to unfold but I like the idea of seeing if the name Miriam Cohen rings any bells with him. If it does seem to ring a bell, we'll see if he brings us back to that summer of '85 and winter of '86 instead of having us lead him there. It would also be interesting to see if he knows that Miriam is no longer alive. If he does know that she's dead, I'd like to see if he can tell us how she died."

"Sheila," said Tony, "this is going to be a tough interview. That's why I would like you keeping notes about what he says and how his mannerisms change or what his body posture tells us. Look for any clues you think might mean that he's lying or trying to hide something. I think you're getting really good at interviewing people and changing direction as needed based on their responses. It would be great if all three of us were able to interview him at the same time, but I think with this kind of a client, Phil has had the most experience in interviewing and that's why I'm going with him. I wouldn't mind doing the interview myself but I think it would be a red flag to Jack Junior that the lead detective was doing the interview. All three of us will need to be on our toes for this one and together we might just get enough information from this interview to really help put this case together."

"Thanks boss," said Sheila. "I was a little disappointed at first that Phil was going to do this interview. I see your point about how experienced Jack Junior is with interviews and that Phil has more experience handling that kind of suspect. I also know that you likely want me to interview Miriam's parents. You know I have had great reservations about that in the past but now that we're sure that Miriam was probably involved, I really would like to take lead on interrogating them. I appreciate your confidence in me watching the interview and picking up on subtle body language that may help us decide when Jack Junior was actually telling the truth and when he was not. I also think that Jack Junior is a better one to interview first because if he remembers about the pregnancy, he may know if her parents were aware of the pregnancy or not, and that would be good information to know going into their interview."

"That's a good observation, Sheila," said Tony. "I thought it was obvious to interview Jack Junior first because he's the one we know for sure is involved with this baby. You've obviously done your homework on how we should go about interviewing Miriam's parents, and that's going to be very important if you are going to get useful information from them."

"Sounds like we have a game plan," said Phil. "I will let you know when Jack Junior gets to the precinct tomorrow. I'll get a feel of him as he gets here and I bring him into the interrogation room. What we can do is, if I scratch my head that will be a signal for you come in to help me instead of staying in the review room with Sheila as currently planned."

Chapter 28

ON **THURSDAY AFTERNOON** Jack Senior and Jack Junior walked into the Newport police station together. They asked to see Detective Hudson and were escorted to his desk. Phil looked up and was more than a little surprised to see them both together, he had not expected this.

"Good afternoon Dr. Del Rio," said Phil. "And this must be your son, Jack Junior, nice to meet you." He led them to the interview room and had them sit down. "I'll be right back," said Phil.

Phil approached Tony with a look of concern on his face. "So much for having everything planned," said Phil. "How do you want to handle this, boss?"

"Well, I am not very happy to interview them together," said Tony. "I suppose this is what we get when we tell him he doesn't need a lawyer. You told me that you did not tell him what this was about; it might be interesting to see the surprise on each of their faces when we mention Miriam Cohen. I hate to break protocol and let the doctor stay with his son during our interview, but I don't see we have a lot of choice at this moment. I think if we tell him he's going to be excluded, Jack Junior will then say," let my lawyer come in instead." Under the circumstances, I think I will just stay in the interrogation overview room with Sheila and will let you handle it by yourself. God knows where we are going to end up with this interview."

Phil ducked back into the interrogation room and sat across the desk from Jack Junior and his dad. "You know that we don't usually interview people with someone present Dr. Del Rio. In this case we're going to allow you to stay but I hope you understand that I will be directing all my questions to your son and I would prefer you let him answer himself."

"I understand," said Dr. Del Rio. "My son is a little sensitive to talking to the police, as you might imagine, so I am just here to support him."

Phil then turned his attention to Jack Junior. "I wonder what you can tell me about a woman whose name is Miriam Cohen?" said Phil. Interestingly, he noted no sign of recognition in either Jack Junior or his father.

"I can't say that I recall that name," said Jack Junior. "Was she an acquaintance of mine or someone who has filed a complaint against me?"

"That's an interesting question," said Phil. "Do you often have people filing complaints against you?"

"No, not usually," said Jack Junior. "In my younger days I was known to rub some people the wrong way. So why or how am I supposed to know this Miriam?"

"Well," said Phil, "we have reason to believe that you knew her in 1985 while you were employed at the Newport Yacht Club." Once again, Phil noted no signs of recognition by Dr. Del Rio, and Jack Junior's facial features now registered mild surprise. Not dismay, just surprise.

"I am still not remembering anything about a Miriam back then," said Jack Junior. "Did I meet her at the marina, did her family have a boat docked there, or did she just come there with friends?"

"We think this is someone you might have had a pretty intimate relationship with," said Phil. He noticed a smirk on Jack Junior's face.

"Well, that may be a list that we don't have time enough to talk to about this afternoon," said Jack Junior. At this point his dad's foot lightly tapped him under the table.

"So, you consider yourself quite the Lothario, is that right?" said Phil.

"I'm sorry," said Jack Junior, a little more chastened this time. "I was pretty wild back then. I know it seems like people never change, but I'm not like that anymore. I spent a lot of time at the marina that summer. Actually I started there in early May and went through September. I was 16 at the time and feeling my oats for the first time. I worked all day and partied all night, every night. I met lots of girls and we had lots of fun. I suppose if you know this much, you've looked up my record from that summer. A few of the yachtsmen filed complaints against me in the club office. In the end, I felt bad about it all because my dad had worked hard to get me the job, and after I screwed it up, I never was welcomed there again."

"So you're basically telling me you had lots of sex with lots of girls," said Phil. "So you may have had sex with this Miriam that I'm asking you about?"

"If she says so, I guess then maybe it's true," said Jack Junior. "Is this some kind of paternity case we're talking about?"

"Not exactly," said Phil. Phil looked at Dr. Del Rio and said to Jack Junior, "I'm sure you've heard about the baby that was found here in Newport several weeks ago." Phil noticed the look of alarm on Dr. Del Rio's face, and also noted that Jack Junior's face registered no surprise. Noting the look on Phil's face, Jack Junior turned towards his father and noticed the look of surprise on his dad's face.

"Dad, what's this all about?" asked Jack Junior. There was a long silence when no one said anything.

"You're telling me that this is about the girl you interviewed me about two weeks ago?" said Dr. Del Rio.

"What you talking about, dad?" said Jack Junior. Jack Senior waved him off, looking intently at Phil. Phil was looking very uncomfortable at this point; this interview had not gone as he had expected.

"Jack," said Phil, "we'll get to your father later. We have evidence that proves that the baby that was recently found in Newport is your child." Phil now noticed that both father and son were in shock.

"So this is about a paternity case?" said Jack Junior. Both his dad and Phil looked at him in disbelief. He honestly didn't get what just happened.

"Detective Hudson," said Dr. Del Rio, "you told my son he did not need an attorney for this interview. When you talked to me last week it sounded like this was going to be a murder investigation. Is my son a suspect in this investigation?"

"Not exactly," said Phil. "He is a person of interest because the DNA of this baby points to him as being the father. We have no evidence at this time that suggests he was involved in any foul play."

"Well," said Dr. del Rio, "I need to talk to my son alone, and please have anyone who's listening in or watching leave us to ourselves."

"Of course," said Phil. "We will give you some privacy and I'll stop back in a few minutes to see what you decided." Phil left the room, picked up Tony and Sheila and they went to the break room.

Chapter 29

"I'M SORRY, BOSS," said Phil. "I think I let that get away from me."

"I think you doing fine, Phil," said Tony. "All this was going to come out in the end and it was very telling to see who responded to what as the interview unfolded. Sheila and I were taking notes next door and as you probably noticed the name Miriam didn't come up on either radar screen when you mentioned her. The question about the job at the Newport Yacht Club registered with Jack Junior but not with Jack Senior. And the reference to the baby found two weeks ago registered with Jack Senior but not Jack Junior. I doubt they will let any more of the interview go on today."

"If they do, do you want to take over, boss?" asked Phil.

"No, I don't," said Tony. "I told you I think you're doing fine and I think if they do let us talk more, you will eventually have to bring up the question about the Buick Riviera. That should really set them off and that will be the end of this interview. At this point I'd rather throw you to the wolves rather than have me go in there and have them biased against me the next time we interview them. If they do let this interview go on, it's either because Jack Junior is really innocent or you convinced them that we have nothing to tie him to the baby's death, which of course is true."

"So you don't mind if they clearly identify me as the bad cop," said Phil. "I see where you're going with this. I have a tiny bit of credibility left at this point but once I make mention of the Buick Riviera, I'll have no credibility at all. I guess it's better for them to think of me that way than to have you or Sheila go in and finish this interview and discredit one or both of you too."

"In addition," said Sheila, "I think the boss is right. You may feel like the interview did not go well but we got some excellent information by their behaviors while it was going on. You might be able to get some more information about Miriam and perhaps her friends. We might need those names if we run into another dead end."

"Okay," said Phil. "I will go in there and be humble. That is of course, if they let me talk to them at all."

In the meantime, Jack and Jack Junior were huddled together in the interview room.

"Dad, do you think we should talk about this here?" asked Jack Junior.

"Well, I don't think they will listen in, if that's what you're worried about," said Jack. "Since we specifically asked them not to listen in on this conversation, anything they heard between us would probably not be admissible if this ever gets to court. First of all, I don't think we should continue anymore of this interview today."

"I don't know dad," said Jack Junior, "it would just make me seem guilty if I asked for an attorney at this point. Don't you think?"

"Well I suppose it matters if you are or aren't guilty in this case. You know by now that you're not smart enough to tell any lies and get away with them."

"Dad, I suspect I met Miriam at the beginning of the summer

but I can assure you I had nothing to do with her after that. I never knew she was pregnant. I never knew she delivered. I don't know what happened to that baby. Besides, how come you seem to know something about the delivery?"

"Well, that's a long story," said Jack. "It seems like a police report I filed a long time ago is what got us to this interview room." Jack went on to give him a thumbnail sketch of those events from 20 years ago. Jack Junior sat quietly, quite bewildered at his father story. He knew that his dad often kept patient confidentiality, but he was surprised a story of this magnitude had never come to light.

"I think we should see what else they want to know at this time, dad," said Jack Junior. "I certainly will now have a hair trigger, and we will pull the plug whenever we think it's necessary."

"Well, don't say I didn't warn you," said Jack. "You have been through the system several times before. You know they're going to want to make a resolution of this case and after 20 years, they will be pulling at straws. You and Donna have a great situation and I don't want even the appearance of you being a scapegoat to ruin that."

"Let's get this over with dad," said Jack Junior. "I can honestly say that I really have nothing to hide in this case."

Jack looked at his son warily. He had no reason not to believe his son now. Of course, if this had been 20 years ago, he would not have been so sure.

Chapter 30

PHIL KNOCKED ON THE DOOR of the interview room and was waved in by Dr. Del Rio.

"Basically, against my advice," said Dr. Del Rio, "my son has decided to let this interview continue."

"I am glad to hear that," said Phil. "I have a few more questions really concentrating on getting to know Miriam Cohen better. Can you tell me a little bit more about what you know about Miriam," said Phil, directing this question to Jack Junior.

"Well," said Jack Junior, "I'm not sure I can place her that summer. Do you have a picture that I could look at or can you give me some more details about why she would have been at the marina?"

"Unfortunately, I don't have a picture of Miriam," said Phil. "So far, we know very little about her and her family. It does not seem likely that they would have had a boat at the marina."

"Do you have an idea of when she would've gotten pregnant?" asked Jack Junior.

"At this point, that maybe a better question for your dad." He turned to Dr. Del Rio and asked, "Can you tell us that?"

"You're asking me?" asked Dr. Del Rio. "I must tell you that this is the most unusual interview I've ever been in on. If I was an attorney, would you direct a question like that to me?"

"No I suppose not," said Phil. There was an awkward silence in the room for a few seconds.

"Well, I guess I would have to say that's she would have gotten pregnant sometime in early May or June of 1985." said Dr. Del Rio.

"Thank you, Dr.," said Phil. At this point the door opened and Sheila hurried into the room and dropped a picture on the table and ran back out. Jack, Jack Junior and Phil looked at each other in amazement and then each study the picture carefully. The girl pictured was thin, with shoulder length hair flipped up at the ends in a typical eighties pattern, her glasses were also dated for the eighties. She looked shy, eyes downcast and the smile was demure. Her blouse had a flower pattern and it was buttoned up all the way to her neck.

"Do either of you recognize this picture?" asked Phil.

"You're asking me another question?" said Dr. Del Rio, he shook his head in disbelief. "The picture is vaguely familiar but you remember I took care of her in the middle of the night and then for two more days 20 years ago. That certainly could be the girl that I took care of that night but I cannot be sure."

"Actually," said Jack Junior, "I do recognize her. But that's not Miriam, that's Mary."

"Mary?" said Phil. "Do you remember her as Mary or do you remember her as the Mary in your dad's story?"

"No, I remember her as Mary," said Jack Junior. He turned to his father and asked, "The girl you took care of was named Mary?"

"Are you guys playing me?" asked Phil. "You mean your father never told you that he took care of this girl 20 years ago and that she was known as Mary Murphy?"

"No, the first I've ever heard of my dad's involvement in this case was a few minutes ago in this very room," said Jack Junior.

"He's telling the truth," said Dr. Del Rio. "My son never knew about this case until today, and he certainly didn't know that the girl's name was Mary."

"So can you tell me why you remember her so well?" asked Phil to Jack Junior.

"I remember so well because she was my first that summer, or actually my first ever," said Jack Junior. "It was my first week at the marina and I met Mary along with her three other friends. They had all just finished their first year at Salve Regina College. Mary and I were both pretty shy but we hit it off that first night of partying. One thing led to another and I ended up rowing her out to one of the unoccupied boats. It was pretty awkward and I think it was her first time also."

"So what happened after that?" asked Phil.

"Nothing," said Jack Junior. "That was the first and last time we were ever together. I only saw her a couple of times in the next two weeks and then not again for the rest of the summer. I never knew she was pregnant and I never knew she had delivered."

"So you got over your awkwardness pretty quickly," said Phil, "because you sound like you had quite a summer for yourself at the marina. You wouldn't happen to know her friends' names would you?"

"Oh yeah, they were the Hail Mary's," said Jack Junior with a smirk on his face.

"What the hell do you mean by that?" asked Phil.

"Well there were four of them. One's name was Haley and the other three were all Marys. Hence the nickname, the Hail Mary's. And of course there wasn't a prayer we could get near any one of them again for the rest of the summer. That was a standing joke among all the dock boys that summer."

"A pretty crude joke, if you ask me," said Phil. "Why do you think you were shut out after that?"

"Because I made a miscalculation. I told her my real age of 16. She was 18, almost 19. They thought I was a sophomore at Providence College and I was just finishing my sophomore year in high school! I ruined it for all the rest of the guys, too."

"Do you remember any last names?" asked Phil.

"No, I didn't get any last names. Why don't you just ask Miriam?" said Jack Junior.

"Well, we would have if we could," said Phil. There was an awkward silence.

"What do you mean by that?" asked Jack Junior.

"I think he means that Miriam, AKA Mary, is dead!" said Jack Senior. By the look on Phil's face, he knew he was right. "When were you planning to tell us about that?"

Phil made a show of squirming in his chair for a few seconds. "We were just getting to that. As best that we can tell; two years after the baby was born, Miriam committed suicide by jumping off the Jamestown Bridge."

"Oh my God!" said Dr. Del Rio. "I remember that case. It was awful. As I remember the story, she was an only child, and the parents took it quite hard."

"I only have one more question for Jack Junior," said Phil, thinking he might get it in while they were distracted. "Were you in the habit of borrowing your stepmother's car?"

"My stepmother and I did not get..."

"Stop right there! What the hell is this all about?" asked Dr. Del Rio.

"There were some skid marks on the bridge that night.

Forensics says they were made by a Buick Riviera. I believe your wife drove that model back then," said Phil.

"This is outrageous," said Dr. Del Rio. "You have been misleading us this whole time. You are now trying to put my son at the scene of Miriam's death. This interview is over and you will hear from our attorney in short order. As a matter of fact, tell your supervisor in the next room that there is going to be hell to pay about this interview."

Jack and Jack Junior got up and left without another word.

145

Chapter 31

"**I LOVE RIGHTEOUS INDIGNATION,**" said Tony, "especially when it comes from a smart and wealthy suspect. Not that the doctor is a suspect, but it gives you the idea we're getting close. Interestingly if he had been Jack Junior's attorney, he would've never made that outburst. Having them both in on the interview was not as bad as I expected. Going in, I thought we might get nothing to work with."

"Oh no, boss," said Phil, "I sometimes find that rich and arrogant people just get like that and it has nothing to do with the case."

"You're right, Phil," said Tony. "But the doctor is not a rich and arrogant person; he's worked his way through the hard times. That's why I specified smart and wealthy people, the ones that had to pull themselves up by their bootstraps to get where they are."

"Overall Phil, I thought that was a very productive interview," said Sheila. "Tony and I were next door and we thought we got a pretty good read on the doctor and his son. I think they know more than they're telling us and the doctors attempts to protect his son were pretty evident."

"Well I think I was a little awkward in bringing up the Buick Riviera," said Phil. "I felt like I jammed it in at the end when I was afraid I was losing the interview."

"No, I think you did a great job, especially when he called you on it and you squirmed a little. He really thought you had made a slip when we had planned that all along," said Tony. "You didn't tell them anything they wouldn't find after a review with the newspapers from back then. It was a big story for several weeks back in the late '80s and I am sure there are numerous newspaper references to it. Sheila, didn't you say that the Cohens have an adopted Korean daughter? It sounds like the doctor doesn't know the family very well because he didn't know that."

"Yes, indeed," said Sheila. "They do have an adopted daughter that I've seen a few times at synagogue. I would guess that she's in her mid-30s so they would've adopted her 8-10 years after Miriam was born. She definitely would have been in the family in the late 80s unless they adopted her as an adolescent after Miriam's death instead of as a baby. Maybe the newspaper articles just never mentioned her."

"That's just my point," said Tony. "If the doctor knew the family well, he would know more than the facts that were in the paper."

"Well I still think we have a few things to do before we interview the Cohens." Phil looked through his notes and added, "I think we can check court records and see if anybody filed a private adoption that didn't go through in early '86. I think we can look at the newspaper articles that were in the paper as Tony suggested in the late '80s when Miriam died. We may also be able to pin down exactly when they adopted their daughter. Sheila, it may be time to call Sr. Jeanne again and see if we can track down these girlfriends with the distinctive moniker of the "Hail Mary's.'"

"Well, overall I think this was a very productive interview. We've established that Jack Junior was somehow involved with

Miriam: and the timing is right to think that Miriam is this baby's mother. We have some things to track down and at least we have some first names about the girlfriends. If we can pin them down as the ones who brought Miriam to the hospital in Providence, then we should be able to get more information if they were involved in the infant's death, or if Miriam was going to put the baby up for private adoption. While we're at it, it's not a bad idea to check with several other agencies in Rhode Island that would have handled regular adoptions like Catholic charities or a Jewish organization that might do the same thing."

"I am not sure there is a similar Jewish organization," said Sheila. "It is very unusual for a Jewish family to give the baby up for adoption. That may have to do with the fact that being Jewish is both a religious and a racial matter. I think most Jewish families would only give a baby up to another Jewish family so we would almost always be talking about a private adoption."

"Good point," said Tony. "So before we wrap this up, is there anything else you think we learned during the interview?"

"The part about the Hail Mary's was very interesting, and Jack Junior sounded completely sincere when he told me that. That part of the story definitely rang true. To carry that over, it seemed like he was also telling the truth when he said he did not know about the pregnancy or the delivery. Guys typically lie about knowing about pregnancies, but if he made up that story about the Hail Mary's on the spot, then we are in really big trouble. He has been interviewed by the police more than most of our suspects, but he has also been burned a few times by them. If he could be that cool, seem sincere in his answers, and make up a story like that on the spot, maybe he's even smarter than his dad."

"That's a great point Phil," said Tony. "I also had the feeling he was telling the truth about the pregnancy. I think you have to balance that with the fact that his dad seemed very interested in protecting him, and I think that just added to making dad sound like he was worried that his son looked or was guilty. What do you think Sheila?"

"I think the fact that Dr. Del Rio came with his son, means that he was concerned about what his son would say with no guidance. I suspect he told Jack Junior to bring an attorney with him, but Jack Junior was worried that would make him seem guilty since we specified he did not need an attorney for this interview. They both seemed genuinely surprised they had both been involved with Miriam at one time or another. Overall, the story Jack Junior gave about meeting with Miriam and that it was the only time they were together certainly rang true for me. Once again, it's very hard to read someone who spent a lot of time being interrogated by the police. Jack Junior says he's changed since those days, and certainly his current family situation would suggest that's true. That of course does not mean he's not guilty of these crimes 20 years ago. I think Phil is right, we need to do a little bit more homework before we go talk to the Cohens."

Chapter 32

DR. DEL RIO AND JACK Junior sat in the offices of Jason Platt. Jason was well renowned in the state of Rhode Island as being the best defense attorney in criminal cases. They spent the first few minutes reminiscing about their previous encounters and Mr. Platt expressed his curiosity at the present situation. He had not seen either of them for 15 + years and the information that had filtered down to him through that period suggested that Jack Junior had turned his life around. He was delighted to hear that it did seem that Jack Junior had settled down with a wife and two children and had not run into any trouble recently.

Initially, Jack Junior did not say much. Dr. Del Rio outlined the circumstances of the case that dated back over 20 years. As he usually did, Mr. Platt said very little and let Dr. Del Rio tell the story. He occasionally raised an eyebrow as Jack and Jack Junior both confirmed that neither of them had any idea that the other was involved in this case. After reviewing his notes for a few minutes, he asked Dr. Del Rio to fill in the timeline for him. Jack told him that his best as could be determined, Miriam had delivered the baby on Super Bowl weekend and then had been admitted to Rhode Island Hospital on the Tuesday of the Challenger explosion January 28, 1986. He and Jack Junior had looked it up, and they had verified that Miriam had likely died on the night two years to the day after the baby had been born.

After pinning down a few more details, Mr. Platt addressed Dr. Del Rio, "well Jack, you know how it goes. I'm going to ask you to leave now because Jack Junior and I are going to discuss some details of this case that I don't want you to know anything about. This is both for his protection and for yours because his conversation with me is privileged and that might not be the case for you. This is especially important since you are a principal in the investigation because of your involvement with Miriam."

"I understand," said Dr. Del Rio. "I trust you completely and of course that's why we are here. Before I leave though, I would like to discuss your retainer, because I want to write you a check today." Jack Junior started to protest but his dad waved a hand at him, "we will discuss this later, and now is not the time."

"Well Jack, my retainer for this kind of case is $5000. As you know, I will subtract expenses as we go along and refund any extra if it wraps up easily. If we have to go to trial, it will probably be significantly more than that. Incidentally, this will be the last time we talk because I do not want them to be able to claim that I prompted you on your testimony. In this case they have a problem because they interviewed you together and therefore established that you might talk amongst yourselves. Let me make it clear that I do not want you to talk to each other about the case anymore."

"Yes, I think I understand the process very well," said Dr. Del Rio. He took out his checkbook and wrote Mr. Platt a check. On his way out the door he gave his son a hug and a kiss on the cheek. "Jack, you know as well as I that you're in great hands. Let's see what we can do to put this behind us."

"So," said Mr. Platt to Jack Junior, "why don't you tell me your side of the story. Please don't leave anything out, and remember that anything you say to me will not get back your father. I know it's been a while since we had to talk like this, but I seem to remember that you became confident in my abilities, and I hope to be able to get back to that point soon."

"First of all Mr. Platt, I'm sorry to have to meet you again under these circumstances," said Jack Junior. "Where do you want me to start and what kind information are you looking for?"

"I would like to hear the story your dad told but in your words, only including the things that you know for sure. I am a little surprised that you never heard of this case from your dad before this week."

"Yes, I was a little surprised myself," said Jack Junior. "It's a hell of a coincidence that we are both involved in this case, and of course the police detectives never believe in coincidences. The beginning and end of my part of the story is that I met Miriam at the Newport Yacht Club. It was the first week I worked there, we got pretty heavily involved that one night and then I basically never saw her again. I never knew that she was pregnant and I never knew that she delivered. I never knew that she was the girl who committed suicide two years later off the Jamestown Bridge. I frankly have given it absolutely no thought until this week and it is shocking to me that the Newport police think I might be involved in the baby's death and then also in Miriam's death."

"Well, you know that that's their job," said Mr. Platt. "I know your attitude about the police is not very good. In your case, you may be a little bit more justified than most young people. I find it helps some people to realize that police are not well paid for what they do, so they demand respect. Lots of people object to that! I know that you understand that since the DNA evidence links you to this baby there is no possibility that you would not be a suspect in this case. I think the first thing I would like to do with you is to establish alibis for both the timeframe of the baby's birth and then also for the night of Miriam's death."

"Well, those are easy tasks," said Jack Junior. "My dad and I looked back at those dates and on the Super Bowl weekend of the baby's birth; he and I were in New Orleans at the Super Bowl! We left to go there on Friday and we did not get back until Monday night. My dad was on call the next day and that's when he admitted Miriam to the hospital. The second dates are even easier. As you remember I served some time for the fire that was set on Halloween in 1985. I served fourteen months at the juvenile detention center in Cranston and I was released in November of 1987. I was then at a halfway house for the next six months. I was allowed to go to school and had limited driving privileges. There was a strict curfew at the halfway house and I had to sign in every night at 11 PM. I then had to sign out every morning at 7 AM when I left for school. We may have to pull up the records and verify the dates, but I am sure at the time of her death, I would have been signed into the halfway house."

"What's the story about the Buick Riviera," asked Mr. Platt.

"Well, it is true that I borrowed my stepmother's car on several occasions. I was a little curious at why they would think that happened but I think I'd been stopped for speeding on several occasions and at least one of those times I was in her car. Of course those episodes were in '85 and '86, before I went to juvenile hall. By the time I get out, my stepmother and I were not on speaking terms and I certainly never borrowed her car in the timeframe when Miriam died. She and dad broke up later that summer and I am sure I was a major reason for the breakup."

"Well, you would not have borrowed her car with her permission, but were the keys available to you so that you might have taken it for a ride?" asked Mr. Platt. "I'm not accusing you, you understand, this is what the police are certainly going to question you about."

Jack Junior remembered what it had felt like to be questioned like this by his own attorney. By now, he understood the process all too well. He also remembered that Mr. Platt had never, ever asked him if he were guilty in any of their previous cases. He had always told Jack that his job was to prove that Jack might not be guilty. "No, I never drove her car in late '86 or early '88. We did initially have a set of rings by the door where car keys were kept, but after I violated my parents' confidence on several occasions, the keys were not kept there any longer. I certainly did not have access to those keys."

"What about the halfway house, did you ever leave after you'd signed in for curfew?" asked Mr. Platt. "Remember, these are certainly questions that are going to be asked by the police."

"Well, I can't say I was in my bed every night while I was at the halfway house. But I can tell you this; I was never caught breaking curfew, so there will definitely be no records of that."

"What about other guests at the halfway house? Were any of them caught breaking curfew and more importantly, did any of them know that you broke curfew on occasion?" asked Mr. Platt.

"I see where you're going with this," said Jack Junior. "Yes indeed, some of my fellow guests did break curfew and were caught. I guess if the Newport police track them down, they would be able to find someone who would testify that I occasionally broke curfew by leaving after signing in."

"That might be a problem!" said Mr. Platt.

Chapter 33

S HEILA STOOD NERVOUSLY on the doorstep to the Cohen home. Phil stood beside her for support. She rang the doorbell and they heard rustling from within. The door was opened by a young woman who stood tentatively surveying them.

"Hello, I am Detective Goldstein and this is Detective Hudson of the Newport police," said Sheila. "You must be Amanda. We have met informally at the synagogue on several occasions."

"Why, yes I am," said Amanda Cohen. "What can I help you with, detectives?"

"We have some information for your parents," said Sheila. "May we come in and are they here?"

"Of course, come on in," said Amanda. "If you wait here for just one minute I will get my parents. Can I ask what this is about?"

"It is a delicate subject that we would like to speak directly to your parents about. You can stay for the conversation if you wish," said Sheila.

A look of concern crossed her face as she left to fetch her parents. She returned a few minutes later with her mom and dad. "These are detectives Goldstein and Hudson," she said as a way of introduction. Her mom looked confused and apprehensive but her dad looked a little defiant.

"What is this all about?" asked Mr. Cohen. "I don't have to tell you how scary it is to have police come to your house. My wife is already upset and you haven't even spoken yet."

"To be completely truthful," said Sheila, "we do have some information that we expect to be unsettling for you both. Is there a place where we can all sit down?"

"Of course," said Amanda. "Let's go into the living room." She took her mother by the arm and led them into the living room where they all sat comfortably facing each other. "

"I am sure you have heard about the baby that was discovered several weeks ago here in Newport," said Sheila. She saw Mrs. Cohen sit up straighter and take more notice, but Mr. Cohen's demeanor had not changed. Amanda continued to sit in a position to support her mother.

"What could that discovery possibly have to do with my family?" demanded Mr. Cohen.

"We have convincing DNA evidence that this baby was your daughter Miriam's child," said Phil. Sheila glared at him. They had discussed this and she had wanted to break this news to the family. She knew that he thought she would be too tentative in bringing up the subject, and she was not happy that he had intervened in this conversation. Still, this was not the place or time to correct him. She decided she was going to go on, but was abruptly interrupted by Mr. Cohen.

"This is outrageous!" said Mr. Cohen. "My daughter Miriam was never pregnant. We have always had a small glimmer of hope that her body would be found and we could put her to rest. We have both been looking forward to and dreading the conversation that would occur, but this information is, well, just outrageous. Your lab has made a serious mistake, and I don't think we need to listen to this anymore."

"I am sorry to have to break this news to you," said Sheila, "but we have information beyond the DNA lab that strongly suggests that this baby was Miriam's. You may not have known that she was pregnant because she received no medical care for the pregnancy here, but she was admitted to Rhode Island Women's and Infants Hospital in Providence for some complications that occurred after delivery. If I could, I would like to direct some questions to Mrs. Cohen and Amanda. Did either of you know that Miriam had a pregnancy?"

Mrs. Cohen slowly shook her head no, tears started to roll down her cheeks. Amanda also shook her head no, "I was here at the time and I did not know that Miriam was pregnant."

"I will not stand by and let my family be questioned in this manner," said an angry Mr. Cohen. "You have answers from both of them. They were not aware of any pregnancy by Miriam and neither was I. We were always a very close knit family and Miriam came home almost every weekend while she was at school."

Sheila looked at Mrs. Cohen who continued to cry and had started to shake a little. Amanda now had her arm around her mom to try to comfort her. She looked at Phil, a little uncertain at what to do next. He quietly gave her a nod of approval to continue.

"There was some confusion at the hospital because the patient gave an inaccurate name. We were wondering if perhaps you knew the names of coeds that Miriam hung around with at college so we could see if we were mistaken about the patient's identity."

"That must be it," said Mr. Cohen. "We were never very happy that Miriam decided to go to that school, and since none of her friends there were Jewish, she never brought any of them here. I suggest you get in touch with Sr. Jeanne Trembley at the school. She has been a great comfort to us after Miriam's death and she might be able to help you solve your mystery." He stood up quickly, moving to help his wife out of the room.

"Of course," said Sheila, "if we could get DNA samples from you both, we could eliminate Miriam altogether."

Mr. Cohen just glared at her over his shoulder. "If you haven't noticed," said Mr. Cohen, "we are done here."

Sheila and Phil also stood up, realizing there was no point in going on with this interview. As Amanda escorted them back to the front door, Sheila slipped her one of her cards and told her to call if she could think of anything else. Amanda started to apologize for her dad's behavior, but Sheila waved her off. "Shalom," Sheila called out to Mr. and Mrs. Cohen. She was not sure they had heard her.

Phil and Sheila sat quietly in the squad car for several minutes before Sheila started it up.

"I think you did real well there," said Phil. "I am sorry I said anything and you were right to wave me off. I won't tell you that these conversations ever get easier, but the questions have to be asked and you asked them. I think Mrs. Cohen knows more than we got out of her today. I am not sure about Amanda though. We know that she was adopted as a little girl into this household, so she was present at the time this occurred. She would have been several years younger than Miriam so it's hard to know how much they would've confided in each other. Still, it's surprising that no one in the family would have noticed Miriam's pregnancy"

"Thanks for coming with me," said Sheila. "I agree with you, Mrs. Cohen knows more than she is telling us. I don't think Amanda knew about the pregnancy but Mr. Cohen's vigorous objections made me wonder if he knows more than he's telling us. Incidentally, I went to college with a girl who wore baggy clothes for a whole year and none of us knew she was pregnant.

In addition, except maybe at the beach in a bathing suit, my mom and dad haven't seen my belly since I was eight years old."

"Good to know," said Phil.

Chapter 34

Jack Junior and his wife Donna sat in the living room of their home in Cranston, Rhode Island. They had spent a typical evening having dinner with the kids, helping with homework and now the children were in bed. Jack Junior had told Donna that they had something important to talk about, and his tone and demeanor told her it would be important.

"You know that I've never kept a secret from you," said Jack Junior to Donna. "We have one to talk about that's going be very unsettling. It's not really been a secret I've kept from you, because I just found out about it myself today."

"You're starting to scare me a little Jack," said Donna. "What can this possibly be about?"

"In the last few days, I found that I probably fathered a child in the late 80s," said Jack. It was painful to see the changed look of Donna's expression.

"You mean to say you have a child in its early 20s? Is it a boy or girl? Where does this child live?" The questions tumbled out of Donna, leaving him a little stunned and not sure where to begin. He sat closer to her and took her hand.

"It's a very sad story," said Jack. "It's going to take me a few minutes to outline all the details, and I will certainly answer any questions you have when I'm done. I had a one night stand with a girl in the summer of '85 when I worked at the Newport Yacht Club. I only saw her in passing a few times after that and then she disappeared from the club and from my life. She evidently got pregnant from that one encounter, and she delivered the baby sometime in January of '86. The craziest part of the story is that my dad then took care of her for complications from the delivery, and no one knew what happened to the baby. The baby that was recently found in Newport was the baby she delivered back in '86, and the police are now investigating what happened. They have some DNA evidence that proves the baby was mine, and I am being treated by them as a suspect."

"Oh my God," said Donna, "what's going to happen?"

"There is more to the story," said Jack. "Two years later, she committed suicide on the Jamestown Bridge. The police are trying to connect to me to her on that night also. They have not accuse me of anything directly yet, but you can probably see where they're going with this."

"Oh my God," said Donna. "What are we going to do?"

"My dad has hired an attorney to work with me for the rest of the investigation. I want you to know Donna; I had absolutely nothing to do with this baby or with this young girl's death. I never knew she was pregnant, I never knew she delivered, and I did not know that she committed suicide. Unfortunately, as you know, I have had some unfortunate run-ins with the police in the past. I am very frightened by the current circumstances. I am sorry I have said nothing about this in the last few days, but I wanted to make sure we had time to sit down and discuss all the ramifications of these events."

"Jack," said Donna, "how are we going to pay for this attorney?"

"My dad is going to take care of it for now," said Jack. "I can't begin to tell you how expensive this might end up being, and for the moment I think we need to let dad help."

"Who is the attorney?" asked Donna.

"Jason Platt," said Jack.

"Oh my God," said Donna. "Jack, he is the most famous defense attorney in Rhode Island. This is really frightening me. Is it possible that you might be convicted on any of these charges?"

"Donna, I am not guilty of anything except meeting this young lady in the summer of '85 and having a one night stand. I certainly had nothing to do with this baby's death and as I said, I certainly had nothing to do with her death. You can understand that my previous involvement with the police is going to work against me. I have all the faith in the world that Mr. Platt will get me through this episode."

"You mean get us through this episode, don't you?" asked Donna.

"Of course I mean us," said Jack. "I am not sure what to tell the kids. If this spirals out of control, and I go to trial, we will probably have to tell them everything. Right now, I am going to hope for the best and that it will not get that far."

"I don't understand what you meant before," said Donna, "your dad was involved in this case also?"

"Evidently, he took care of her after she delivered. Neither of us had any knowledge of our involvement until I was interviewed by the Newport police. From what I can determine, it was dad's call to the police departments of Providence and Newport that led them to who this patient might be. Even if my dad had not been involved at all, the DNA evidence on the baby would have led the police to me, but my dad's role and her trip to the hospital might have never come to light."

"So what does your dad have to say now?" asked Donna.

"That's just it," said Jack, "my dad and I can no longer talk about this. Since he will be involved because of the phone calls he made to the police, Mr. Platt does not think that he and I should collaborate on information any longer."

"That's terrible," said Donna. "I know from your past how helpful your dad could be in this kind of situation. I hope this doesn't mean we can't talk to him about our kids, or have him over for dinner."

"I'm confused about that myself," said Jack. "I think as long as we don't discuss this case, I would like things to go on as before. We have a lot to lose with this situation and I don't want our relationship with my dad to be one of them. As you might imagine, ignoring this topic is going to be difficult!"

Chapter 35

PHIL APPROACHED THE front door of the Arnold residents in Mystic Connecticut. He was a little apprehensive as this was an unscheduled visit because he had been unable to touch base with Suzanne Arnold in all his previous attempts and he was getting suspicious he had been getting the run around on purpose. He rang the doorbell and it was answered by a strikingly beautiful young woman who looked to be of Korean descent. She had on what was apparently a school uniform so it was evident to him immediately that she was not part of the help. "Good afternoon my name is Detective Phil Hudson of the Newport police," said Phil.

"Oh, were my parents expecting you?" asked Melissa Arnold.

"No, they were not expecting me to come today," said Phil. "And you might be?"

"Oh, I am Melissa Arnold," said Melissa. "Is this about that baby that was found on one of our properties?"

"So you know about the case," said Phil.

"Of course I do. We have been talking about it a lot. My mom is especially upset that this would've happened on one of our properties," said Melissa.

"Who is it dear?" asked Suzanne Arnold as she turned the

corner into the foyer. She's stopped short, not recognizing the gentleman standing in the doorway. "Excuse me, who are you?"

"I am Detective Phil Hudson," said Phil.

"Was my husband expecting you?" asked Suzanne. "He's on his way home but not here yet."

"I just have a few questions I would like to ask you and your husband," said Phil.

"I don't understand," said Suzanne "was he expecting you or not?"

"Actually, no. I was in this area on another case and thought I would stop by."

"My husband will be home shortly," said Suzanne, "and we have decided that we would not talk to the police again without our attorney being present. If you don't mind waiting in the library for a few minutes I will bring in him when he comes home."

Suzanne dismissed her daughter Melissa with a subtle headshake and led Phil into the library. "Please make yourself comfortable," said Suzanne. "Would you like something to drink while you wait?"

"No, I am fine, thank you very much," said Phil. "I had a few questions just for you, like whether you were ever in the house where the baby was found?"

"I guess I didn't make myself clear," said Suzanne, "I will not answer any more questions until my husband gets here."

Phil made himself comfortable on one of the armchairs near the fireplace. Despite little chill in the air, there was a fire in the fireplace. There were bookshelves on all four walls and virtually every space was taken up with a book. The dark wood paneling and the Oriental rugs that his chair sat on spoke of the money that the Arnold's obviously had. 35 minutes passed before Mr.

Arnold opened the door and walked into the library with another gentleman.

"What is this all about?" asked Mr. Arnold. "I find it highly unusual that we have made several communications in the past, I've had my attorney forward you all the document you asked for, and now you show up at my home unannounced."

"I'm sorry," said Phil, "as I explained to your wife, I was in the area and decided to drop by to get more information directly from your wife about how well she knew the house in Newport and whether she remembered any unusual tenants from there."

"Strangely just driving by; Mystic Connecticut is at least an hour and a half away from your Newport precinct. This visit was unannounced but I think you came here deliberately to try to talk to my wife and daughter without me or counsel being present. I think I ready told you that this was a house from my childhood, and not hers. I also told you that she did not deal with my father's real estate business, and she did not remember any tenants from that era. From now on I want to be sure you direct questions to me or my attorney."

"So you mean I can't talk to your wife?" said Phil. "And who exactly is the gentleman standing near you?"

"You are correct, I don't want you to talk directly to my wife without me or my attorney being present," said Mr. Arnold. "This is our family attorney, Mr. Howard Baines. He provided you some of the information you had requested about the tenants in the Thames St. house. I must tell you that this kind of an unannounced visit suggests you are treating us like suspects."

"No, you're not suspects," said Phil. "Since you and Mr. Baines are here, can I talk to her now? Should you be suspects?"

"No, I think you have asked enough questions today and even I don't need my attorney to tell me not to answer the second question," said Mr. Arnold. "I will have my maid, Eileen, show you back to the front door."

"Thanks for your cooperation," said Phil. He smiled at Mr. Baines as he left, and Mr. Baines smiled back.

Chapter 36

JACK SAT ON HIS BOAT waiting for the roar of Sally's car to announce her arrival. She was a little later than expected, so he was nursing his second single malt scotch. Luckily the casserole in the oven would keep until she got there. When she arrived they quietly ate dinner, and Sally was concerned that his preoccupation of last week had carried over to this week. They usually talked once or twice a week while she was in Vermont, but there had been no communications this week. Their lovemaking that night was passionate and playful, as usual. Sally did however note an occasional misplaced sigh that signaled that Jack was preoccupied with other thoughts as well. Still, she was as satisfied as usual when they were done and she fell asleep shortly after he did.

The next morning during breakfast, Sally finally got Jack to open up about his week. "Jack, what on earth happened this week because, if anything, you are quieter than last week?"

"Jack, Jr. was interviewed by the Newport police because he evidently conceived the baby with the girl I took care of postpartum. It's an unbelievable coincidence!"

She was shocked that the bizarre story that had unfolded the week before had become even more bizarre with the angle involving Jack Junior. Jack's concern about exposing a young woman to an event more than 20 years ago had turned into even greater concern about his son's possible involvement in the case. Miriam's death confounded the problem and Jack expressed concern that his determination in involving the police had distracted his ability to understand that this traumatic event might have led to her death. "Maybe if I had been more supportive of this young lady and less accusatory, she would not have ended up committing suicide. The possibilities are endless and I have lost a lot of sleep this week running them in my head." Even when Sally pointed out to Jack that he had reverted completely to his role as physician by the second and third day of Miriam's hospital stay, he remained unconvinced that if he had done more it might have been a different outcome.

"I have never quite seen you like this before," she told him. "I am concerned that your distraction about your care to Miriam will detract from your ability to assist Jack Junior at this critical time."

"I see your point. Thanks! All my current efforts will be directed to helping Jack Junior."

Jack had decided not to sail this weekend so they spent time on the boat at the dock. Jack continued to outline his plan to have Mr. Platt represent Jack Junior from now on. Sally was alarmed to hear that Mr. Platt did not want Jack or Jack Junior to talk about the case anymore. Jack recounted on how this has been helpful in previous times when Jack Junior was in trouble. As directed by Mr. Platt, Jack would direct any thoughts or possibilities directly to him and not to Jack Junior.

"Will you be able to compartmentalize these conflicting duties?"she asked Jack. His look at her became distant and as the weekend progressed, she felt more and more left out of the

172

conversation. He knew that she had been annoyed in the past when Jack seemed to dismiss her from assisting in other parts of his life. They both knew they shared a different and special relationship that most couples would not understand. She was unhappy that in his most difficult week of their relationship, he had shut her out. She had been busy and not called him but he had not called her either. As their conversation about Jack Junior's troubles petered to almost nothing, she had a final thought as the weekend came to a close.

"How was Susie this week?" asked Sally as she closed her car door. Jack's stunned facial expression and verbal aphasia told her all she needed to know. She drove away in silence.

Chapter 37

"**O**KAY BOYS AND GIRLS," said Tony, "where are we now?"

"Well I'll be darned," said Phil. "This has become the most confusing case I think I've ever worked. The best suspect we have, Jack Junior, seem sincere in his answers and I don't think he did it. On the other hand, the Cohens and the Arnolds get more secretive all the time. They do behave like they're guilty. I just don't know what they're guilty of."

"Well, let's break it down and tell me what you got," said Tony. "Let's start with you Sheila."

"Well, Phil and I interviewed Mr. and Mrs. Cohen together. Their daughter Amanda was also there, comforting her mom during the interview. Mr. Cohen was defiant the entire time. No one expressed any idea that they knew Miriam had been pregnant. I think Phil will concur that he and I both thought Mrs. Cohen was not truthful about that. I think they were all quite rightly shocked that instead of telling them we had found Miriam's remains, we might have found the remains of Miriam's baby."

"I think Sheila has it right," said Phil. "Even when it became awkward, she was able to ask the questions we needed to know. We even requested better DNA samples than the one Mrs. Cohen had provided in the search for her daughter's remains, but we were shot down about that also."

"So you mean you got to meet Amanda also," said Tony. "What was she like and did you get any answers from her that were helpful?"

"Well I told you I have met Amanda several times before," said Sheila. "We had checked and found that she had been adopted as a baby from Korea by the Cohens when Miriam would have been seven or eight years old. As I remember her from synagogue, she was very supportive of her mom at a time that was very emotional for her mom. She denied knowing about the pregnancy, and we decided that with the seven or eight year age spread between her and Miriam, they might not have been sharing what would have been very sensitive information."

"We both agreed that Amanda probably did not know about the pregnancy," said Phil. "We also both agreed that we think Mrs. Cohen probably did know about the pregnancy and we were split on Mr. Cohen. He protested so much and was so aggressive in his tactics that I thought he might have been trying to hide something."

"Could you get an impression about if anybody knew what happened to the baby?" asked Tony.

"Well to be honest boss," said Sheila, "it never crossed my mind to ask them about that." She looked tentatively over at Phil.

"Wow, boss," said Phil, "we never even got close to asking that question."

"I understand," said Tony."What about your interview with the Arnolds, Phil?"

"If anything, that was an even more difficult interview than the one with the Cohens," said Phil. Sheila looked at him with a bit of skepticism on her face. "I showed up at their house unannounced, because I was tired of not getting any answers directly from Mrs. Arnold. I met their adopted daughter, Melissa, and Mrs. Arnold greeted us a few seconds later. Melissa was very welcoming and probably a bit naïve, but Suzanne Arnold was very unhappy at my visit. She immediately directed me to the library where I sat cooling my heels for more than half an hour until Mr. Arnold showed up with his attorney. Mr. Arnold let me know in no uncertain terms that it was unacceptable for me to show up unannounced. Since this suggested we were treating them like suspects, he was no longer going to respond to any requests to talk to him or his wife without his attorney being present. He made it perfectly clear that if we wanted any other information about the house on the Thames Street, we would probably need a subpoena."

"I suppose we should not be surprised that he didn't buy your driving by scenario when you stopped at their house in Mystic, Connecticut. Sounds like you got to speak to Suzanne and Melissa Arnold for a few minutes before her husband intervened. Did you get any useful affirmation out of them?" asked Tony.

"Not really," said Phil. "Looks like Melissa is probably a junior or senior in high school, so she would be 17 or 18 years old. That means she would not have even been born when this case occurred. Incidently, she is also Korean by birth.

"Mrs. Arnold seemed tightly controlled with her answers. It sounded like she's been coached by her husband and attorney. I wouldn't say that she was rich and arrogant but rich and privileged probably fits the bill. I specifically asked her if she'd ever been to the house on Thames Street or remembered any tenants there, but she politely refused to answer."

"How was Mr. Arnold?" asked Sheila.

"What do you mean by that?" asked Phil.

"Well, did you get the impression he's knows more about this case than he has let on in the past?" asked Sheila.

"Or did you get the impression he's trying to protect his wife?" asked Tony.

"Let me think for a minute," said Phil. "I think there's a little bit of both things going on. What surprised me more was that he seemed to be protecting his wife. We have discussed the angle that Miriam gave her baby up for adoption; maybe we should look at the Arnolds as someone she might have known."

"Well, as you both know, early on we asked the Cohens if they knew the Arnolds and they said no. Sounds like a direction we need to pursue," said Tony. "Maybe we need to ask the Arnolds if they know the Cohens! What else you guys have on your agenda for now?"

"Well, I'm going to talk to Sr. Jeanne and see if I can get a connection on Haley and the two Mary's that were Miriam's friends. When I e-mailed her last week, Sr. Jeanne suggested that the trio did not come to mind. She told me that she would talk to some of the other faculty members and see if they could come up with some names. She did tell me that they were three Haleys and 12 Marys enrolled in just Miriam's class so that sounds like too many to just start calling at random. I also checked into adoption records around the beginning of '86," said Sheila, "several filed and went through, but I did not find any that were filed and then abandoned."

"Boss, I think the next thing with Jack Junior is to check on his alibis," said Phil. "As we previously discussed I suggest you handle that interrogation and you know that he will have his attorney present."

"Yeah, I guess it's time for me to start doing some work," said

Tony. "Let's see if we can set up that interview in the next few days."

Chapter 38

JOAQUIM DEL RIO JUNIOR and his attorney Jason Platt sat in interview room one. Antonio Fuentes made his way into the room and sat down across the table from them. They all made the necessary introductions.

"I guess you know why you're here," said Tony. "As you know, we're trying to make a decision about whether we should consider you a suspect in this case. You are now fully represented by Mr. Platt and I'm going to proceed with my questions. Why don't we start by having you tell me what you know about Miriam?"

"I am afraid I don't know a whole lot about Miriam. I knew her as Mary. I told your fellow detective, Mr. Hudson, exactly what I remember from that time," said Jack Junior.

"Yes I have notes about what you told him, but I'd like to hear it for myself," said Tony.

"Okay," said Jack Junior. "I met a girl named Mary in the early summer of 1985 at the Newport Yacht Club. I was working there as a dock hand, and she came by with several girlfriends. We were both pretty shy at our first encounter but one thing led to another and we were able to get alone and we had sex. I saw her two or three more times after that and then she sort of disappeared for the rest of the summer. I never knew her real name was Miriam

Cohen, I never knew she got pregnant, I never knew she had a baby, I never knew the baby died, and I didn't know that she herself died two years later."

"We have reason to believe that she delivered on Super Bowl weekend in early 1986. Can you tell me where you were at that time? I know it may be difficult because it was such a long time ago," said Tony.

"Actually, not at all," said Jack Junior. "My dad and I had traveled to New Orleans for the Super Bowl that pitted the New England Patriots against the Chicago Bears. We went out there on Friday night and we got home on Monday night."

"That's a pretty good alibi," said Tony. "I suppose you have some documentation or witnesses that can corroborate your story."

"Well, my dad can corroborate my story," said Jack Junior. "We obviously met a lot of people there that weekend, but you'd have to ask my dad how to get in touch with them."

"Did you know any of the girls that Mary/Miriam was with when you met her?" asked Tony.

"I had just met them the same day I met Mary. I saw them around the marina for most of the summer but I was persona non grata with them after that initial encounter."

"You told Detective Hudson it was because they didn't realize how young you were when you first met. Is that correct?" asked Tony.

"That's what I told Detective Hudson," said Jack Junior, "but you'll have to ask the girls if that's why they didn't associate with me after that first week."

"You mean after that first week or after that first encounter?" asked Tony.

"Yeah, what I meant to say was after that first day's encounter with them, they never spoke to me again."

"What about the other dock boys; did any of them know who they were better than you did?" asked Tony.

"I don't think so," said Jack Junior. "I guess you can ask some of them if they could identify them better than I can."

"That's a good idea," said Tony. "Can you give me the name of the other guys you worked with that summer?"

"One was Armando Almeida and another was Manny Costello. They had both worked there the summer before, but I don't think they knew the girls from that summer. I don't think the girls had much to do with them during the summer of '85 because they gave me a hard time telling me that I had ruined their chances with the girls after that first week."

"What about your supervisor?" asked Tony.

"That was Howard Adams. At first I thought he was just going to be a hard ass, but he treated me and the boys pretty well. A couple of times he told us to knock it off when he heard about the late night parties with the girls but we did our work and he appreciated that."

"I thought you told me you didn't party with the girls after the first night?" said Tony.

"Oh I mean the other girls. Armando, Manny and I had a pretty good time that summer. There were a lot of other girls there that were our age and we got along better with them," said Jack Junior.

"Okay Jack," said Tony, "what about two years later in January of 1988. Can you tell me where you were on the night of January 25?"

"Do you mean the night of January 25, the morning of January 26 or the night of January 26?" asked Jack Junior.

"I mean the night of January 25 that became the morning of January 26," said Tony. "Are you trying to be cute with me?"

"No," intervened Mr. Platt. "Jack Junior wants to be as cooperative as possible with this investigation. I can assure you he was not trying to play with you." He signaled Jack to continue.

"I had been released from the correctional facility about six weeks earlier and I was residing at a halfway house on those nights," said Jack Junior. "I spent a total of 6 months at the halfway house."

"So you mean you are at the halfway house on both the 25th and the 26th, is that right?" said Tony

"Yes," said Jack Junior.

"Tell me more about your stay at the halfway house," said Tony.

"I was able to attend school and I had a part-time job but otherwise I was signed into the halfway house with an 11 PM curfew and I couldn't leave before 7 AM the next morning," said Jack Junior.

"So if I check into the records I will find that you did not miss any of your nights of curfew?" asked Tony.

"Correct, you will not find that I broke curfew while I was there for the six months," said Jack Junior.

"Were you actually there every night or are there just no records to prove you were not there?" asked Tony.

"I'm not going to let him answer that," said Mr. Platt.

"Why not," asked Tony. "It's a legitimate question to confirm his alibi."

"But if he admits to breaking curfew, that means he violated his parole. I'm not going to let him answer that question," said Mr. Platt.

"Let's change the subject then. Tell me if you had access to your stepmother's car during the month of January 1988?" asked Tony.

"I did not have access to my stepmother's car. By that time we were not on speaking terms. I didn't drive my father's car during that time either," said Jack Junior. He was bumped on the elbow by Mr. Platt, and he remembered that he was not supposed to offer information that wasn't asked for.

"So how exactly did you get around? Did you have a driver's license and was it limited in any way?" asked Tony.

"I had this crappy X-11 Chevy that was almost 10 years old. My driver's license had never been suspended, but part of my probation did not allow me to drive between midnight and 6 AM. I was told that if I had been stopped, it would violate my probation."

"So your stepmother will confirm that you did not have access to her car?" asked Tony.

"I have no idea what my stepmother will say. She hates my guts, and if she thinks it will get me in trouble, she might say I did drive her car. She thinks I broke up her marriage with my dad, and she's probably right that I did play a big part in it. But it was her who did not want my dad to help me and she was furious with him when he wouldn't stop. They had broken up completely by the summer of 88," said Jack Junior.

"Can you give me the names of some of the other people who stayed with you at the halfway house?" asked Tony.

"No, I can't. I have tried to put that episode out of my mind. I'm sure the authorities there can give you all the information you need to know," said Jack Junior.

"I want to thank you both for coming in," said Tony. "We're obviously going to have to check out your alibis, and if I need more information from you I will contact you both."

They all stood up and shook hands and Tony had one last thought, "I have one last question."

Both Jack Junior and Mr. Platt stood straight up, knowing this was a typical tactic that might throw them off their game.

"You know that we are worried that Miriam did something that resulted in the baby's death. Do you think she could have done that?" asked Tony.

"Mr. Fuentes, I knew Miriam for about 12 hours. We were both kids. I don't know how anybody could kill a baby and I'm not sure I knew her well enough, but I don't think Miriam could've done that!" said Jack Junior.

"If that's all," said Mr. Platt, "we're going to leave now."

"Thanks again for your help," said Tony.

Chapter 39

JACK LISTLESSLY DROVE to his apartment in Providence. Jack Junior and Donna had told him they had other plans for tonight so he was not going to make his usual stop in Cranston. He wondered if this was somehow connected to the fact that Mr. Platt did not want him and Jack Junior to discuss the case. He wondered if it was acceptable for him and Jack Junior to talk about how they weren't going to discuss the case. Jack felt like his whole life had turned around in the last two weeks. First there was the unsettling news about the Newport police finding the baby from two decades ago. Then there was the even more unsettling news that his son Jack Junior was involved in the case. Now, his distraction with the case was driving a wedge between him and Sally. Sally had always known about his arrangement with Suzie and indeed with several others before her. Jack somehow had the feeling that this latest breach with Sally was much more serious than any that had come before. When he got into his apartment, it was quiet and dark. He checked her room and found that Suzie had already gone to bed. He was grateful that he did not have to deal with her tonight, as he was not sure he could check the emotions he was feeling after Sally's abrupt departure. He quietly went to the master bedroom and took a long shower. As he was getting dressed for bed, Suzie cracked his door open, said she'd heard him coming, and asked if he was okay. When he told her he was fine, she quietly went back to her room after they made quick arrangements to meet for dinner Monday night.

Jack sat up in bed carelessly listening to the 11 PM local news. He had 100 thoughts churning in his brain, and after 15 minutes he realized he had not heard a word from the TV and he shut it off. He reflected on how one day 20 years in his past could make such an incredible difference at this time. He had known at the time that it was going to be a significant event in his life; he had always thought that it would someday have another impact, but he never dreamed that it would so thoroughly involve his son as part of the drama. He desperately wanted to believe that his son had no involvement with Miriam after their first encounter. Certainly he understood quite convincingly that his son was not capable of doing anything like that now. He knew that one day he would again be confronted by questions from the Newport detectives, and he silently prayed that he would not say anything that would endanger his son's credibility with the police. He had complete faith in Mr. Platt. Mr. Platt's ability to work well with Jack Junior, even in the times when Jack Junior had been guilty, had always meant that the punishments were fair and that's all you could really ask for. The validation of his trust in Mr. Platt was borne out by the current circumstances of Jack Junior's life. He knew that his daughter-in-law Donna had known about Jack Junior's escapades before they got married. He silently hoped that this new episode would not negatively impact on their current strong relationship.

Jack diligently went about his work at the clinic for the next three days. He'd always had an uncanny ability to not allow his private life interfere with his medical duties. He and the residents and medical students continued their strong working relationship, and they were able to deal with multiple diverse medical problems for the patients that came to the clinic. He had a quiet dinner with Suzie, discussing her dreams and aspirations for when she finished her current academic duties. At this point in their relationship they could talk about anything. This intimacy, more than their sexual escapades, would probably have been even more damaging to his relationship with Sally, had Sally known about it. Once Suzie graduated and moved on, they would probably keep in contact, send Christmas cards, and talk on the phone. The conversations would be frequent at first but inevitably trail off to once or twice a year. At least, that had been the usual course of events with previous tenants. Suzie, Jack and Sally all knew that eventually, someone else would rent out the back room.

Chapter 40

MR. AND MRS. COHEN and Amanda Cohen and their attorney, Jack Holtzman, all sat in interview room number one.

"Hi, I am Detective Antonio Fuentes," said Tony, "I am the lead detective in this case. I see that you brought your attorney with you, I'm not sure that was necessary."

"The hell it's not," said Mr. Cohen. "It sounds like you're trying to pin this baby's murder on my daughter. Even though she's dead, I'm not going to let you dishonor her in this way."

"I'm sorry you feel that way," said Tony. "You have to understand we need to follow the evidence as it comes before us. If your daughter was alive we would not be accusing her of anything, just trying to get the facts of what happened to this baby."

"I don't believe you," said Mr. Cohen. "That's why we brought our attorney with us. For all I know, you think my wife or I had something to do with this baby's death."

"That's an interesting comment," said Tony. "I don't think that's crossed any of our minds before you just mentioned it." This seemed to have the influence that Tony was hoping for, as Mr. Cohen then sat quietly for a few minutes. Tony turned his attention to Mrs. Cohen "I was wondering if you could tell me in your own words what was going on with Miriam at this time. Do you think she was capable of hiding a pregnancy from you?"

Mrs. Cohen looked dolefully at Tony. Her daughter Amanda held her hand and encouraged her. "I don't think she could have hidden the pregnancy from me," said Mrs. Cohen.

"So you're saying she didn't hide the pregnancy from you?" said Tony.

"I'm not sure I like this line of questioning," said Mr. Holtzman. "My client is obviously very distressed by this situation and it sounds like you're trying to lead her with your questions."

"I'm sorry," said Tony. "What I really want to know Mrs. Cohen, is whether you knew that Miriam was pregnant in the Fall of 1985 and gave birth in early 1986."

"No I didn't" murmured Mrs. Cohen, her eyes averted to the table.

"I'm not sure what you said," said Tony.

Mrs. Cohen looked at him defiantly in the eyes and said, "I never knew that Miriam was pregnant!"

"What about you Amanda, did you know..."

"No, no, no," said Mr. Holtzman. "You did not request that Amanda come today and she is only here to support her mother. If you insist on asking her more questions, we're going to reschedule the rest of this interview."

"Oh, I don't mind," said Amanda, "I didn't know..."

"No," said Mr. Holtzman, "you are not going to answer any questions today. Do you have any more questions for Mr. and Mrs. Cohen?"

"We understand that Miriam had three friends at Salve Regina College. As far as we can determine, there was a girl named Haley and two girls named Mary," said Tony. "Could you help us identify who they were?"

"I am sorry to report," said Mr. Cohen, "that my wife and I were not very supportive of Miriam's attendance at Salve Regina College. I think because of that, she never felt comfortable about inviting her friends to come to our home. Sad to say, we never really got to know those people she was friendly with."

"We think these girls may have invited her to join them at the Newport Yacht Club. Might that help you better identify who those friends were?" asked Tony.

"I don't think so," said Mr. Cohen. Turning to his wife for the first time he said, "Does that jog any memories for you?"

"No, they don't," said Mrs. Cohen. "I am sorry but as my husband has described, we were not as much a part of our daughter's life as we should have been at that time. Maybe if we had been, the events two years later would not have happened." She seemed to shrink before Tony's eyes and Amanda gently put her arm around her.

"One last question, "said Tony, "and this one is going to be difficult. Two years later the official ruling was that your daughter committed suicide. You both seem reluctant to accept that at the time. Was there something specifically suspicious you were or still are concerned about?"

"I'm sorry you had to bring that up," said Mr. Cohen. "I suppose no parent ever feels that their child is capable of committing suicide and my wife and I are no exception to that rule. I can't speak for my wife, but over the years I have come to the conclusion that our suspicions of foul play were probably unfounded." He looked at his wife who slowly nodded her head in the affirmative. She added no more comments.

"Well I thank you for coming in today," said Tony. "I know this has been a very troubling time for you and I'm sorry to bring up old memories. That's all the questions I have for now."

"I have a question," said Mr. Cohen. "Earlier you asked about the Newport Yacht Club. Does that mean you have an idea about who the father of this baby might be?"

"I am sorry to say I have no information that I can give you at this time," said Tony. "I can assure you that when we complete this investigation, we will give you all the information we have that involves Miriam."

"Thank you," said Mr. Holtzman. They all got up and left the room.

Tony sat with Sheila and Phil. "I think Mrs. Cohen knew about the pregnancy and maybe more, "said Tony.

"Or, she was feeling guilty she did not know her daughter was pregnant!" said Sheila.

"There is that," said Tony, "good point!"

Chapter 41

SHEILA ONCE AGAIN parked her car outside the administration building of Salve Regina University. She made her way up to Sr. Jeanne's office and was ushered in. She and Sister Jeanne exchanged pleasantries and Sheila got right to the point. "Sister Jeanne, I was wondering if you could help me with the names I supplied to you?" said Sheila.

"I'm afraid I have not come up with any more information for you. As they told you over the phone there were three Haleys and 12 Marys in Miriam's class here at the college. I had my secretary go through the classes that Miriam attended as a freshman here and we never came up with a valid combination of names that seem to fit the bill. I spoke to several other faculty members and that combination didn't ring any bells for them either. We looked into Miriam's dorm room assignment for her freshman year and once again her roommate or the coeds in the rooms around her did not come up with a combination that made sense. I'm not sure where to go from here."

"Sounds like you did a lot of background checking for us, sister," said Sheila. "It seems to me that no matter how we go about this, if we just start inquiries into the people from her class, it would quickly get around and might let these parties get away from us."

"I suppose talking to the Haleys first would make sense since there were only three of them," said Sr. Jeanne. "Can we be sure that they would be classmates of Miriam that we are talking about?"

"I'm not sure what you mean, sister," said Sheila.

"Well if we expand to the two classes ahead of Miriam, we are up to five more Haleys and 20 more Marys. We did look into the one class that Miriam took with upperclassmen, but no one from that class stood out. They were only a few other Jewish students at the school in Miriam's freshman year, and none of them were named Haley or Mary."

"Do you remember any students that might have had connections with the Newport Yacht Club?" asked Sheila.

"I suspect I could more easily give you a list of students that didn't have some kind of connection to the Newport marinas," said Sr. Jeanne.

"Let's take a different tack," said Sheila. "We have interviewed the Cohen's mom and dad and sister, Amanda. My partners and I all get the idea that we think Mrs. Cohen knew about Miriam's pregnancy. You said she has stayed relatively close to the college here, and I was wondering if you could remember anything that would make you think that she knew that Miriam had been pregnant or had a baby?"

"That's a difficult question," said Sr. Jeanne. "I feel like I am betraying Miriam's memory and her mother's trust in me as a representative of this University. As I consider your question though, I don't remember any conversations that I've had with Mrs. Cohen to suggest that she knew anything about her pregnancy."

"Is there anyone else on the faculty or administration that she might have divulged the information to?" asked Sheila.

"Wow, I am again uncomfortable with this question," said Sr. Jeanne, "but I don't think there is anyone else here that she is remotely as close to as she is to me."

"What about Mr. Cohen?" asked Sheila. "Might he have said anything along these lines?"

"No, I am sure that is not a conversation that I ever had with him. Most of the time he comes with his wife for support, he doesn't engage in conversation, he smiles politely and shakes hands but he is clearly not as comfortable with this relationship as his wife is," said Sr. Jeanne. "Even when they gathered here on campus for the one-year remembrance of her death, I remember him saying virtually nothing to all the people that attended."

"You held that one year remembrance service here on campus?" asked Sheila.

"Yes we did," said Sr. Jeanne. "As you probably know, Jews that commit suicide are not usually allowed to be buried in the Jewish cemetery. That was certainly complicated by the fact that Miriam's body was never found. Jewish tradition then usually has a gathering one year later to dedicate a headstone, but the Cohens could not come up with a way to do that in the traditional Jewish manner. They were quite upset about it as the year anniversary approached, and I suggested we might have a remembrance here on campus. Mrs. Cohen was delighted with that idea and even Mr. Cohen warmed up to it pretty quickly. They had already discussed starting a fund in her memory, and I suggested we dedicated a plaque of some kind here on campus on the anniversary of her death."

"I guess I didn't know about the suicide rule," said Sheila. "I know that the year anniversary is a solemn tradition in the Jewish religion and it is wonderful that you could accommodate that tradition here on campus."

"Many of their friends attended and even the rabbi stopped by for the plaque dedication. She had been well known on campus and many of her fellow classmates attended as well," said Sr. Jeanne. "There were more than 300 signatures in the remembrance book by the end of the day."

"So there is a record of the people who visited her memorial on that day?" asked Sheila. "Maybe I will ask the Cohens to look at that to see if we find a combination of people that match one Haley and two Marys signing together. It would not surprise me at all that if her friends attended, they would come together."

"Actually, you don't have to ask the Cohens about that book," said Sr. Jeanne. "It is in the library beside the memorial plaque to Miriam. It is referenced on a wall sign near the wall plaque and visitors are encouraged to sign it even now. Some of the money donated by the Cohens over the years has been used to put together several copies of Jewish literature and holy books including a Torah. I know that Mrs. Cohen stops by yearly on the anniversary of Miriam's death to see what books we've added to the collection and to see if there are new entries into the remembrance book. Surprisingly, even after all these years, we still see a new name added every once in a while. When we are done here, I will show you how to get to it."

"That would be great," said Sheila. "The last question I have before I leave is if you remember anyone who might have dated Miriam while she was here?"

"I have thought about that too," said Sr. Jeanne, "but I don't ever remember Miriam hanging around with guys. I take it then that you have not found the young man who might be responsible for this pregnancy?"

"I am really not at liberty to discuss that with you," said Sheila, "but in strict confidence I can tell you I do think we have found him, and he had no relationship with the college."

"Thanks for sharing that with me, Sheila," said Sr. Jeanne, "and I can assure you that particular piece of information will not be released by me to anyone unless you tell me it's okay."

"Well then," said Sheila, "I'm ready to go visit your library."

Chapter 42

PHIL RE-FILLED EVERYONE'S coffee and rejoined them at the table. They had just completed discussing several other cases and were going to compare notes on the Newport baby case. Phil and Sheila took out the folders that were getting thicker by the day. Phil started off.

"I have pretty much finished looking at all the tenants that rented the house on Thames Street and I haven't come up with anything. Most of the tenants had multiple kids and the house would've been pandemonium all the time. The documentation I received from Mr. Arnold suggested that the keys were changed on a regular basis and it doesn't look like old cleaning services or repair men would still have had access to the house in its final stages of repair after the Arnold's left. Assuming the baby was interred shortly after the weekend of January 25, 1986, the house would've been between tenants at that time. I checked one more time with the coroner, and he says the staining on the newspaper that was present with the baby suggested the burial was right around the time the paper was published. I asked if he thought the baby may have been kept somewhere else and then transferred to the location on the Thames Street, and he said he didn't think so. Since the Arnolds live in Connecticut and have done so for a very long time, I checked adoption records in Connecticut as well as here in RI and I found no instances in which adoption papers were filed and then canceled here or there. Incidentally, I was curious and I found out that their attorney, Howard Baines, is registered in both Rhode Island and Connecticut."

"Wait a minute," said Sheila, "did you say their attorney was Howard Baines? That is the adoption attorney that Sr. Jeanne referred me to. I have already talked to him about common practices for private adoptions in Rhode Island in the late '80s. Can that be a coincidence?"

"Good work people," said Tony. "I think we're going to have to pursue that a little bit more. They either have nothing to hide or it's pretty brazen of them to introduce him to Phil after he had talked to Sheila. Maybe you catching them by surprise in Connecticut is going to yield more than we thought."

"I think I have some other good news," said Sheila. "The more I work with Sr. Jeanne, the more helpful she becomes and the more insightful she becomes. Seems they had a memorial service for Miriam one year after her death at the campus. She let me review the remembrance book that was signed that day and I found the configuration we were looking for. The book was signed by Mary Brady, Haley Quinn, and Mary Bennett, in that order. I was so excited after that find, I ran back to Sr. Jeanne's office and when I showed her those names, she did seem to remember that they were classmates of Miriam who might have spent time with her. We then pulled class records and each of those three girls had multiple classes with Miriam when they were freshmen at the college in '84-'85."

"That's great," said Tony, "now we know exactly who to interview without letting the gossip mongers scare away the real suspects."

"Isn't it a little hasty," asked Phil, "calling them suspects already?"

"I think we need to get this investigation moving," said Tony. "I think if we treat them as suspects from the beginning, they won't beat around the bush about what their relationship with Miriam or this delivery or this baby or its death was. If they think we can charge them with something, I don't mind shaking them up and threatening them with the responsibility of his baby's death!"

"That will certainly do it," said Sheila. "What do you think the chances are we can get them all in here at the same time? We can each interview one of them, and maybe even let them see that we're interviewing the others?"

"I like it boss," said Phil. "Let's see if we can do that."

"Might be good to see how much contact they still have with each other," said Tony. "Of course we could try a little subterfuge, and get them here under false pretenses. You know, someone broke into their car or we found some jewelry they'd reported missing."

"I think that's a bad idea boss," said Phil. "You are obviously getting frustrated because I've never seen you so willing to piss people off."

"We're policemen Phil," said Tony, "we will do what we have to do."

"I think we just all try to interview them at the same time, even if it's at their homes or work. That way even if we don't get anything," said Sheila, "we could check their cell phone records after we've been there. If there are nonstop phone calls back and forth between them all, we will know that we are on the right track."

"Okay then," said Tony. "Let's see if we can figure out where they are at any one time and we may be able coordinate talking to them at the same time."

Chapter 43

JACK SAT ON THE fantail of his boat and struggled with his emotions. He was nursing his second half tumbler of single malt scotch. It was late afternoon on Friday and he was feeling sorry for himself. Sally had called earlier in the day to tell him her students had a major project due on Monday and that several had asked her to help them. She was not going to make the trip to Rhode Island this weekend. Although she sounded upbeat and matter-of-fact on the phone, Jack could not tell if the recent events with Jack Junior's accusation and Sally's feelings he had excluded her had made his escapades with Suzie less palatable to Sally. She had seemed very unhappy with him when she had left last week. Still, she had confirmed that she expected this to be a one weekend deal and that there was no doubt in her mind she would come down the following weekend. Jack looked around forlornly. He had planned to sail to Martha's Vineyard this weekend, one of Sally's favorite trips. It was still early September and you could never tell when that trip would no longer be feasible. Certainly, he could make the run to Martha's Vineyard or even to Nantucket well into November, but the cold breezes were not particularly comfortable and he had long ago decided he had nothing to prove with these sailing trips. At least he could be comforted by the fact that Donna had called him and invited him to dinner on

Sunday night at their home in Cranston, so he felt there was some improvement in that relationship. He and Donna had briefly spoken about the rules involving what he and Jack Junior could talk about, and he felt the plan to only discuss current family events would work well. He was certainly looking forward to seeing his grandchildren once again this weekend.

Jack went into the galley and laid some nautical maps on the table. His mind quickly calculated times and distances to various locations. Although Sally was a great help when he sailed, he could certainly handle the boat by himself if necessary. In the final analysis he decided he would not sail this weekend. Jack put the nautical maps away and pulled out some roadmaps. He carefully plotted a road course to the MGM Grand Foxwoods Casino in nearby Connecticut. Since the forecast for the weekend was good weather, he decided he would ride the Road King there. He carefully poured the second half of his drink back into its decanter. If he went out to dinner at 6:30 and he would hit the road around 8 PM, he was sure that he would not be alcohol impaired for his trip. He enjoyed his motorcycle trips into Connecticut because as long as he assiduously avoided Route 95, most of the other secondary roads in Connecticut were perfect for cycling.

He took several minutes to call ahead and make a reservation for Friday and Saturday night at the MGM Hotel. He was assured that they could accommodate him with a tee time at the Isles North course late Saturday morning. He would have to rent clubs at the course since he couldn't travel with them on his motorcycle, but he didn't play golf often enough to be married to one particular set. He would occasionally bet a $25 or $50 Nassau with whatever partner he was assigned with, and you realize that losing that was part of the cost of entertainment for the weekend. He would probably spend some time at the gaming tables, but excessive gambling had never been a problem for him. He always had his limits and could stick to them. He also booked a massage at their spa for late Sunday morning.

Jack got some chowder and clam cakes from the outdoor window at George's in Galilee. He walked across the parking lot and found half of an empty table overlooking the inlet that separated Galilee from Jerusalem. It amused him to think that his boat was docked approximately half a mile away from where he sat but he had driven approximately 9 miles to get here. He watched a parade of boats that went in and out of the inlet. There was the regular large ferry to Block Island. There was the fast ferry to Block Island there were fishing boats, and there were private watercraft. Some boats were going in and some boats were going out. All cruised very slowly in the no wake zone, so you could get a good look at each boat. Who were the crew, who were the passengers, what equipment was on board, which one was seaworthy and which one should stay inside the breakwater? Like other people who were people watchers, Jack was a boat watcher. On occasion you could see the Coast Guard cutter scrambling from its position just north of the Salty Brine State Beach. It would carefully make its way through the Narrows and it was always inspiring when it opened up its engines and got on plane to get to the open ocean. It was magnificent to watch each crewman carry out their designated duties. Jack always checked the newspapers the next day to see if he could decide what the emergency had been. Time and time again as he read a sad story, Jack was comforted by the fact that he had put in the time and effort to learn his sailing capabilities. As with many other things in life, many sailors knew what they were capable of, but few took the time to realize what they were not capable of. In most cases, tragic outcomes came from people who had never learned that lesson.

When Jack got home he took a few minutes to go through his motorcycle checklist. He was really proud of his brand-new Harley Davidson Road King. He had slowly graduated, over the last 12 to 15 years of riding, from the first Dyna Low Rider to the Softtail Heritage Classic to the current Road King. He prided himself on how well he took care of his various modes of transportation including his car, his motorcycle and his boat. Jack had avoided getting the Bluetooth connection for his helmet, so when he was on the road, he was truly unreachable. When he rode his bike, he got the same sensation he had had in the operating room; he was busy and he should not be disturbed. The tires looked good, there were no frayed wires and the belt was properly tensioned. There were no oil leaks visible on the ground underneath the parking space. He rapidly checked lights and turn signals. A check through a saddlebags verified that his rain gear was properly stowed even though there was no expectation of rain for the weekend. Since he was going solo, he could pack his duffel bag and seat it snugly on the passenger seat of his bike. A few tie-downs kept everything in place. Jack carefully pulled out of his parking space in Snug Harbor and carefully made his way out to Route 1 S. and followed his handlebar mounted GPS system that had been carefully set to stay on secondary roads. As was always the case, he was attentive to his driving and to his surroundings on the road. He comfortably made it to Foxwoods in less than two hours.

Jack checked into his room and changed out of his riding gear. He spent an hour in the casino, getting slightly ahead at the blackjack table and then losing it all at the roulette wheel. He sat at the bar watching the late news and finished his second single malt Scotch of the night. He slept in Saturday morning before taking the hotel shuttle out to the golf course. He got placed by the starter in a group of three retired local surgeon's whose usual fourth was sick today. The four had chatted about the new business directed model of medicine and they lamented the loss of the old days. None of them were interested in betting, so there was no Nassau to wager on this day. Jack quietly shot an 86, not too bad for someone who only played 8 to 10 rounds each summer and was using rented clubs. Jack later met his new friends for dinner and spent another hour and a half at the casino. He slept in on Sunday morning and made his massage treatment. His trip back to Snug Harbor on the motorcycle was uneventful and he quickly showered and changed and jumped in his car for his trip to Jack Juniors'. Earlier in his life, Jack would've considered this a lost weekend but now, in his mid-50s, he recognized that weekends like this were sometimes necessary to recharge your batteries. He was feeling pretty serene as he drove to Jack Junior's house, definitely looking forward to hugging his son and grandchildren and to eat whatever wonderful meal Donna had put together for that evening.

Chapter 44

A T TWO O'CLOCK on Monday afternoon, Phil entered
the real estate office where Mary Brady worked. Before he
entered her office, he had been able to see her at her desk, and
he had just gotten off the conference cell phone call with Tony
and Sheila who were about to confront Mary Bennett and Haley
Quinn respectively. He approached the receptionist and asked if
he could speak to Mary Brady. He did not show his badge at this
time because he wanted the receptionist to think he was simply
another real estate client. He told the receptionist his name was
Phil Hudson and she brought him to Mary's desk and introduced
him. After the receptionist had left to go back to her desk, Phil
carefully showed Mary his badge and asked, "Is there somewhere
private that we can talk?"

Mary's reaction was immediate and telling. She cast her
eyes down and said to Phil, "Yes we can use the office upstairs."
As Jack followed her upstairs, he realized that she was trembling
slightly. They went into the room just to the right of the top of
stairs and she waved him to a chair, she closed the door behind
herself and sat across from him. "What can I help you with
officer," she said quietly.

Phil, Sheila, and Tony had decided they would all use the
same opening line. "I am sure you have heard about the baby

that was found in Newport three weeks ago, that's what I'm here about," said Phil.

Although she was trying hard to remain calm, Mary was clearly distraught by this pronouncement. "How can I possibly help you with that case?" asked Mary.

"I was wondering if you had any theory about how the baby may have ended up in that house on Thames Street?" said Phil.

"Why would you think I would know anything about that baby?" asked Mary.

"We have it on good authority that you were friends with a coed at Salve Regina College named Miriam Cohen." Phil noticed Mary stiffen almost imperceptibly. "We have DNA proof that the baby was Miriam's." He sat quietly for a few seconds, waiting for her to make the next move.

"Yes, I was Miriam's friend. We supported her through her pregnancy, but none of us were there when she had the baby. The first thing we knew about her delivery, was when she came to us two or three days later telling us that she had been bleeding heavily and was now feeling feverish. We took her to the Newport emergency room and then accompanied her to Providence."

"When you say we, who do you mean?" said Phil.

Oh," said Mary, "you don't know who the others are?"

"I'm not here to play games," said Phil. "We know at least two others in your clique but we want to know if there were more."

"No there were just the three of us and Miriam. I'm uncomfortable telling you who they were," said Mary.

"Haley Quinn and Mary Bennett," said Phil. Once again he said nothing more because he wanted Mary to go next.

"Okay, so you know all of us," said Mary.

"I want you to tell me what you know about what happened to the baby after it was born and shortly thereafter. Keep in mind that this baby has now been found dead, so you should choose your words very carefully."

"Do I need a lawyer?" asked Mary.

"Do you need a lawyer?" asked Phil. "I guess if you're guilty you need a lawyer but all I want to do is find out how this baby ended up where it did."

"I already told you," said Mary, "we were not around when Miriam delivered her baby. We only helped her when she was in trouble several days later."

"We have a witness who says that after Miriam was confronted about the baby's whereabouts, the people who had brought her Providence disappeared. We certainly think that was you and Haley and Mary."

"Yes, we did bring Miriam to Providence," said Mary. "We did not abandon her there because we were feeling guilty; we had to get back to school so we contacted her mother to go see her in Providence."

"Wait a minute," said Phil. "Are you telling me that Miriam's mother knew about her pregnancy?"

"Yes, her mother certainly did know about the pregnancy," said Mary. "Maybe if her mother lied about knowing about the pregnancy, she had something to do with the baby's disappearance."

"Are you telling me that Miriam and her mother conspired in this baby's disappearance?" asked Phil.

"That sounds like a good theory to me," said Mary.

"Wow, you're pretty quick at throwing her mother under the bus. Sounds like a theory, or you know it as a fact?" asked Phil.

"A theory," said Mary, "I told you I don't know what happened to the baby."

"I have another question for you," said Phil. "We think Miriam may have given this baby up for adoption. Do you know anything about that or if there was someone Miriam might have given the baby to?"

"I don't have any idea about any adoptions," said Mary.

"So you are sticking to your theory that Miriam and her mother disposed of this baby?" asked Phil.

"I'm not saying that", said Mary, "I really don't know what happened to the baby."

"Do you know who the father was?" asked Phil. Mary shook her head no but said nothing. "Do you know why Miriam might want to kill herself two years later?"

Mary was mute. Her expression suggested to Phil that she would not answer any more questions. "Can you tell me..." he stopped as her slow shaking of her head announced that this interview had ended.

Phil gave her his card, and asked her to call him if she could think of anything else. She assured him she would call him and ran out of the room.

At the same time that this interview was taking place, Sheila was talking to Haley Quinn and Tony was talking to Mary Bennett. When the three detectives met back at the precinct in Newport, they compared notes and realized that all three interviews, with only slight variations, had been eerily similar. The consensus was that all three women agreed that they had known Miriam, that they had known about her pregnancy, and that they had not been present for her delivery. None of them knew what happened to the baby. They had assisted her in going to both the Newport and Providence hospitals. They all agreed that Mrs. Cohen definitely knew about the pregnancy. None of them were willing to accuse Miriam and her mother of disposing of the baby, but none of them could come up with a different reasonable explanation. They all categorically denied that they knew anything about a plan to give the baby up for adoption. They all had said they did not know who the baby's father was and all the detectives thought they were lying about that because of the information they had from Jack, Jr. They all had thought Miriam had become more depressed before her death but none knew why. Phil, Sheila and Tony all recognized that a confrontation with Mrs. Cohen was now inevitable.

Chapter 45

TONY AND PHIL looked on in shock as Mrs. Cohen was escorted to Sheila's desk. They saw pleasantries exchanged and then Sheila got up to take Mrs. Cohen to interview room one. Sheila subtly signaled to Phil and Tony to go into the review room. Sheila and Mrs. Cohen said across from each other at the interview table.

"Can I get anything for you like a coffee before we start?" asked Sheila. Mrs. Cohen solemnly shook her head no. "I want to thank you for coming in to speak with me today but I want to be sure that you do not want your attorney to be here with you."

"I am fine," said Mrs. Cohen. "From what you have told me, you know that I lied about knowing about Miriam's pregnancy. My husband never knew about the pregnancy, and I would like to keep my knowledge about it a secret if possible."

"I can promise you discretion," said Sheila, "but depending on where this investigation takes us, your husband may find out all the details."

"I also know I could've brought in my attorney," said Mrs. Cohen. "I'm not sure where his loyalty lies and since I feel like I have nothing to hide, I don't think I need to have him here."

"You realize that it is not legal to lie to a police officer don't you?" asked Sheila. "Of course if you do, you know that you have already lied to us."

"I would hope you understand the impossible position I was in, with both my husband and my daughter present at our last interview," said Mrs. Cohen.

"I understand," said Sheila. "Why don't we just proceed today and see how it goes. Why don't you just tell me about Miriam's pregnancy?"

"I realized about the pregnancy when she was 4-5 months along," said Mrs. Cohen speaking softly and slowly. "You might find that very unusual since she visited home very frequently during that first semester of the '85-'86 school year. I had noticed that she was quieter than usual and she had not been as interactive with her sister as she had been prior to this time. I confronted her about the pregnancy; she made me promise that I would not tell my husband. When I told her that put me in a delicate position she said that if he found out she would insist until her death that it was her idea that I not tell him. In my wildest dreams I never realized her death would come so soon." Sheila sat quietly as Mrs. Cohen took several minutes to recompose herself.

"What can you tell me about the delivery?" asked Sheila.

"Surprisingly, I can't tell you much. Miriam insisted that she was going to take care of it herself even though I begged her to see a doctor. She evidently had made arrangements for a home delivery with a nurse midwife and she told me that she had found a great home for the baby to go to. When I pressed her for details, she told me that she knew I would grill her about the details and that is why she had tried to keep knowledge of the pregnancy from me. Her accusatory tone made me feel ashamed, so I dropped it."

"So you're telling me that Miriam gave her baby up for adoption," said Sheila.

"Yes, as far as I know! The next I heard, I was being called by her friends in Providence saying that she had gotten into trouble after the delivery and had needed emergency surgery," said Mrs. Cohen.

"Do you know the family she gave the baby up to?" asked Sheila.

"Unfortunately, I never did find out who it was. She assured me that it was someone she had known for a while, that the couple would make great parents, and I got the impression that they were somehow related to one of her girlfriends at the college."

"This is very important information for us to find out about," said Sheila. "You understand that this baby died only three or four days after birth so we would consider the adoptive parents suspects in the death of this baby."

"You cannot believe how ashamed I am that I did not offer my daughter more support. I have always blamed myself for the circumstances that spiraled out of control, leading to her suicide two years later," said Mrs. Cohen.

"So did you know that this baby had died? If you did know, do you know if Miriam knew?" asked Sheila

"I'm ashamed to say that I did not know the baby had died, but in retrospect, Miriam's behavior in the next two years would suggest to me now that she did know about the baby's fate. I realized that she was slightly depressed in the spring of '86 but she was putting on a brave face and as a parent I want to believe she was fine. She seemed a little down in January of '87 but nothing would have led me to believe that she would take her own life in January of '88."

"I know you continue to publicly state that you don't think that Miriam committed suicide," said Sheila. "What if I told you we were looking into the possibility that her death involved foul play?"

"I don't want to hear anything about that unless you are absolutely sure that someone else is involved. Privately, I have resigned myself to the fact that I lost my daughter in January of 1988 and nothing that I do or say or anyone else does or says will ever bring her back."

"I'm sorry to have brought that up," said Sheila. "We're going to keep looking into the death of the baby. There is one last thing I must ask you, do you think there is any possibility that Miriam had anything to do with the death of the baby and that she was feeling guilty about that?"

"I can't believe you would even ask me that," said Mrs. Cohen. "I will only tell you one last thing. On two occasions I asked Miriam if she knew how the baby was doing and in both instances she smiled sadly at me and said it was doing better than could be expected under the circumstances."

"Thank you so much for coming in today, Mrs. Cohen," said Sheila. "You helped a great deal and I am sorry to have put you through this ordeal, especially since your daughter did not accompany you for support." Sheila escorted her out and then joined Tony and Phil in Tony's office. They all sat quietly for a few minutes looking dumbfounded.

"Well," said Tony, "I guess we ran into some well rehearsed alibis by the Hail Marys. Sounds like one of them is protecting a family member but we will have to figure out which one because she will never give that up. I think if we interrogate the right one of the three, we will be able to shake out what we need to know, the truth."

"It sounds like the relative was someone that Miriam already knew," said Phil, "so I think if we eliminate the local coeds, we should interview any of the three that came from out of state."

"Sounds like a place to start," said Sheila. "I will check with Sr. Jeanne to see who was local and if someone was not local. We can also check on the local girl or girls about nearby family members."

"Incidentally Sheila," said Tony, "nice job at getting Mrs. Cohen here by herself!"

Chapter 46

As Tony arrived at the precinct, he noticed Phil and Sheila huddled together at Phil's desk looking at a file folder. Curious, he walked over and asked, "What's going on?"

"I had a folder delivered to me just before I left last night," said Phil. "It's from the secretary of the Providence Chief of Police. I spent several hours looking at it last night and I asked Sheila to join me here early this morning so we could look over its contents. You are not going to be happy chief!"

"I'll have to hear it sooner or later," said Tony. "So you might as well let me have it."

"You might want to be sitting down," said Phil. Tony's grimace told him everything he expected about how this information would go over. "Jack Del Rio is the father of Miriam's baby."

"Yeah, so tell me something we don't know," said Tony as he turned in his chair to look at Sheila who looked breathless. "I think we established a few days ago that Jack Junior was the baby's father."

"Dr. Jack Del Rio is the baby's father." Phil and Sheila watched as Tony's face turned scarlet.

"Holy fuck!" said Tony. "See, I told you all along that this case was not going to be good. Exactly what kind of evidence do we have that Jack Senior is the father of the baby."

"We have an affidavit from the Providence police DNA lab that a DNA sample from Dr. Jack Del Rio matches Miriam's baby in a pattern that confirms that he is the father of the baby, not simply the grandfather."

"Wait a minute," said Tony, "I am not a doctor but how can Jack Junior and Jack Senior both be this baby's father? And where the hell did they get a DNA sample from Dr. Del Rio?"

"Well, if you remember, I was told that Jack Junior had a 96% likelihood of being the baby's father. This affidavit seems to contradict that information; it confirms that Jack Senior is the baby's father. There is no explanation of how that is possible. They got Dr. Del Rio's DNA from a bone marrow bank that he contributed to when one of his friend's children came down with leukemia."

"Is that even legal?" asked Tony. "Scratch that. We'll have to cover that later. Do you realize how complicated this case just became? We have been thinking we were so smart to let the doctor sit in on his son's interview, and we have managed to give away all the advantage we had because he knows now where we are headed. First of all, tell me why the office of the police chief in Providence is trying to help us with this case?"

"Sheila and I have been thinking about that," said Phil. "What we think is going on is that the police chief's brother is the officer that Dr. Del Rio spoke to on that night in January 20 years ago. I've made a few calls and it seems like the chief's brother is about to retire. His having ignored the call 20 years ago is a scandal he doesn't need on his service record when his retirement is being contemplated."

"I guess I'm a little dense," said Tony, "but isn't this just going to highlight the difficulty Dr. Del Rio had that night?"

"We figure they are thinking that this is going to come to light anyway," said Phil, "so they're trying to bring this information to light to put a negative spin on Dr. Del Rio even before it hits the presses. It gets better, Tony, we're not even half done in telling you what this folder tells us."

"Okay, give me the rest of the bad news," said Tony. "I obviously have a lot more questions to ask but maybe I need to hear it all before I can formulate anything intelligent."

"Remember that Dr. Del Rio told us that he was in trouble with hospital administration because he accepted this patient without proper authority?" said Phil. "Well it seems the doctor left out another important investigation that was occurring at this time. It seems that there was a nurse midwife that worked in his office who was ultimately found not to have any medical license. As a matter of fact, all her scholarly credentials were false. During the investigation of his office it came to light that the nurse midwife had been involved with several private adoptions, some of which may have been illegal."

"I don't like the sound of this," said Tony. He looked at Sheila who shook her head in disbelief.

"Well, the illegal part may have been that the office was hiring young girls, getting them pregnant, and then paying for them to give the baby up for adoption."

"Okay so far," said Tony, "I still don't see where that leaves us with Dr. Del Rio?"

"He along with the other doctors in the office were all investigated but no charges were brought against them. But, there are several allegations by the police in this report that suggested that perhaps Dr. Del Rio had gotten some of the girls pregnant himself!"

"Holy shit," said Tony. "I don't believe it. I always thought I was a pretty good judge of character, and I find it hard to believe that the doctor we've spoken to several times would be involved in something like that."

"What if I told you the doctor is currently living with a 22-year-old nursing student and their relationship is not considered to be platonic," said Phil. Tony looked at Sheila who was nodding her head yes.

"So this theory would be," said Tony, "that the doctor got Miriam pregnant, she backed out of the deal, the doctor disposed of the baby and then when Miriam started to crack, the doctor disposed of Miriam. Is that what we're thinking?"

"I can tell you I'm having a hard time wrapping my head around this one boss," said Sheila. "The problem is that when we have looked into these scenarios and allegations, there certainly was an investigation and Dr. Del Rio definitely has an eye for younger women, even now."

"Here I thought we finally had a breakthrough. We may have found a way to see who Miriam gave the baby to, and now we have a new suspect we've never even considered before. Suspects, witnesses, and alibis are coming fast and furiously. It's enough to make your head spin," said Tony.

"Oh by the way," said Sheila, "just so you know we didn't drop that ball, I spoke to Sr. Jeanne and it seems that Mary Brady had a cousin named Suzanne Brady whose current name is Suzanne Arnold. A little more digging brought out the fact that Suzanne had been a babysitter for Miriam when she was a child. That would explain how they knew each other, why Mrs. Cohen may not have known the Arnold name and how that ties into the baby being found at the Arnold house."

"I hate to say it, but you know I don't believe in coincidences," said Tony. "The problem is this case has so many coincidences, some of them have to be just that, coincidences. I think we need a little bit more proof on both the Arnold angle and the doctor angle. One of you should interview either Haley Quinn or Mary Bennett and see if you can pin down this Suzanne Brady connection. We can threaten them with obstruction if they don't cooperate. Phil, let's look into this possible illegal adoption ring and see if we can tie Dr. del Rio into it. Let's see if they ever found out what law firms were being used and we'll pray to God that the Arnold's attorney was not part of it."

"I'm a little confused," said Phil. "What would it matter if he was involved in that adoption ring?"

"He is going to come to an interview as the Arnold's attorney," said Tony. "Do you see a way we can turn the tables on him and drag him into this case as a suspect who may have known about the baby's demise?"

"That's a tough one boss," said Phil, "have you ever had to deal with that scenario before?"

"No I haven't," said Tony. "I know you told me you checked for adoption papers that were filed and rescinded. Let's check the records in Connecticut since that is where they live and I will bet you Mr. Baines has a license there also. And while you guys are chasing down those connections, I am going to talk to the district attorney to see how the hell we're going to pursue all these leads, especially if the attorney is involved."

Chapter 47

PHIL SAT ACROSS the desk from Haley Quinn. She looked nervous. It was not a surprise visit this time; he had called her in advance to make an appointment. He sat quietly for a few seconds watching her get more nervous, which is exactly what he intended.

"Haley," said Phil, "we have a witness that absolutely confirms that Miriam had planned to give her baby up for adoption. In the last interview we had, you told us that you knew of no such plans. I would remind you that it's illegal to tell a lie to a police officer so I am here to let you redeem yourself."

"I don't know what you're talking about," said Haley. "I told you that I knew about Miriam's pregnancy and that I, along with some of my friends, tried to help her. We were not present for her delivery and only went to the hospital with her when she got in trouble two or three days later. She never told us that she had planned to give her baby up for adoption."

"Well then, what did she tell you she was going to do with the baby?" asked Phil.

"She never really told us what she was planning to do with the baby," said Haley.

"Wow, you have to do better than that," said Phil. "Do you really expect me to believe that you guys helped her with the pregnancy and helped her after her delivery when she got in trouble but she never confided in you what her plans were for the baby."

"It may not sound true," said Haley, "but it is the truth."

"All right, let's change the subject for a second, "said Phil. "Do you know who got Miriam pregnant?"

"I think it was a boy she met at the Newport Yacht club in Newport Harbor the weekend after we finished final exams of our freshman year," said Haley.

"Now we are getting somewhere," said Phil, "that may be the first fully truthful thing you've told me today. Our investigation has pinpointed who that was, and we not only think he may have had something to do with the death of his baby, we also think he may have something to do with Miriam's death." Phil tried hard not to bite his tongue as he made these statements since he already knew these statements might not be completely true. "You can see where we might be able to charge you with obstruction after the fact. Same for Mary Brady and Mary Bennett. The one who sings first gets the best deal."

"I see your point," said Haley. "We had all made promises to Miriam and to each other about what we would say if we were ever discovered. We were all petrified after the doctor confronted Miriam in the recovery room and we spent days waiting for the ax to fall. Miriam had decided to give the baby up for adoption and Mary Brady told her about her cousin Suzanne who had been diagnosed with infertility. Miriam knew Suzanne because Suzanne had babysat her, and she had contacted Suzanne directly for the arrangements. The three of us were not involved with delivery, that part is true. We heard that the adoption was off because the baby was stillborn and we only got involved again when Miriam ran into trouble with the bleeding. After that, we were never as close to Miriam again although we did hang out on occasion and we all realized that Miriam was probably a little depressed during the next two years. Just as she seemed to be getting better, Miriam died that night on the bridge. We were all shocked at that. After Miriam's death, especially when there was a question of foul play, we were once again petrified we would be suspects. When the investigation implied that her death was a suicide, we all sat down with Suzanne and agreed there was no reason to bring her into the situation. We had carefully planned our cover story but never had to use it until recently."

Phil had been carefully scribbling notes as Haley spoke and he acknowledged each new revelation with a shake of his head. "Thank you very much Haley," said Phil. "I know this hasn't been easy for you and I am glad you recognize that this story was never going to hold up to intense scrutiny. If you can think of anything else you want to add, please call me. I will call you if we think of anything else to ask."

"Am I in trouble here?" asked Haley. "Can I expect some charges to be filed against me?"

"I honestly cannot answer that question," said Phil. "After we are done with the full investigation, we will give information to the district attorney who will make a decision about how to proceed."

Chapter 48

Tony and Sheila sat across the desk in interview room number one, facing Suzanne Arnold and her attorney, Mr. Howard Baines. It'd been a major accomplishment to get this interview set up because Mr. Arnold had insisted he be present. Since Sheila had already interviewed Mr. Baines, she had spoken directly to him about why they needed to interview Robert and Suzanne individually. Robert had also been concerned that they would not allow Mr. Baines to represent both of them. Even after Sheila had pointed out to him why that was not a good idea, she had consulted with Tony and they had decided to grant that request. Since Robert and Suzanne were husband and wife, they could not be made to testify against each other in any case. Tony had already considered that if they each had a different attorney, it might be easier to bring charges against Mr. Baines. His conversation with the district attorney had suggested that that was going to be a stretch under any circumstances. In any case, these wranglings had confirmed to Tony that Mr. Baines and the Arnolds knew more than they had told him.

"I'm not going to lie to you," said Tony, "we now have connections between you and Miriam, you and the house where the baby was found, and witnesses that will verify that Miriam had arranged for you to adopt her baby after delivery."

"I told you that I had nothing to do with Miriam's pregnancy, the death of her baby, or its burial in the house on Thames Street. I will acknowledge that I knew that Miriam was pregnant. My cousin Mary told me that Miriam was looking for a family to adopt the baby. I did have a conversation with Miriam about that, but it never went anywhere. The next I knew, I had been told that the baby was stillborn and that any hopes of this adoption were gone. My husband and I had had infertility for five years and we were concerned about engaging with Miriam on a plan for adoption. We knew that after delivery, plans like those often fall through. I did not want to face that possibility," said Suzanne. "Despite my efforts, I was devastated for months after that." Tony could see the great effort that Suzanne had put into this confession and he asked her if she needed to take a break. She shook her head, no.

"It has certainly been suggested to us that you were helpful to Miriam at the time of this delivery. You are saying that you had nothing to do with this delivery," said Phil.

"I think she very clearly answered that question," said Mr. Baines. "Considering how difficult this is for Mrs. Arnold, I will ask you not to change the wording of a question that has already been asked and answered."

"I think you have to admit the fact that this baby was found buried in a house owned by the Arnold family. That is a coincidence we have to pursue. You have told us that you had no knowledge of how the baby ended up in the house on Thames Street. Do you think your husband can answer that question?" asked Tony.

"I'm not going to let her answer that question," said Mr. Baines. "You're asking for her opinion/knowledge about what her husband did or knew, and that is not acceptable."

"I'm sorry," said Tony. "I guess I can ask that to Mr. Arnold

234

himself. I don't think I have any more questions for you at this time. Thank you for coming in."

Tony turned to Mr. Baines and asked him if he wanted to take a minute before they interviewed Mr. Arnold. Mr. Baines replied by escorting Mrs. Arnold out of the room and bringing Mr. Arnold in.

"Your wife Suzanne just told us that although she knew about Miriam's pregnancy, she had abandoned plans to go through with an adoption. So the adoption never occurred. Is that your understanding of the situation?" asked Tony.

"I had heard rumors of a potential adoption, but unlike my wife, I wasn't sure about the infertility and I still thought we could have our own children. I heard later that the baby had been stillborn and I tried my best to keep my wife positive about getting pregnant herself." said Mr. Arnold. "Unfortunately that never happened and as you know we have a beautiful adopted daughter. My wife never got over not having our own children and I have tried hard to dispel the notion that this baby was one that we lost. You can see how distressing these inquiries have been for my wife."

"As I explained to your wife, Mr. Arnold," said Tony, "since the baby was found in a house owned by your family, I really had no choice but to pursue these inquiries. While we're on that subject, do you know how this baby ended up where it did?"

"I have no idea how the baby ended up in that house," said Mr. Arnold. "If I knew it was there, do you think I would have allowed workers in that basement to find a body that would inevitably involve police investigation?"

"I see your point," said Tony. "I actually have only one more question. If you had pursued this adoption, would Mr. Baines have been your attorney?"

"I don't have to answer that question," said Mr. Arnold. He immediately got up and started for the door.

"He doesn't have to answer that question," said Mr. Baines. Mr. Baines glared at Tony and Tony smiled back at him. Howard took a second look and Tony was still smiling. Tony had made his point and a now chastened attorney left the room with his client.

After a minute, Phil joined Tony and Sheila in the interview room. "Boss," said Phil, "that was quite a set of interviews."

"I can tell you I was petrified to speak," said Sheila. "And I wasn't even the one being interviewed. Nice dagger at the end there at Mr. Baines, I think he got the point."

"Sounds like the DA told you to go slow with that angle, boss," said Phil. "I see you chose not to mention that the baby was not stillborn."

Tony smiled, "Some bullets you shoot and some you keep in the gun. Someone, or maybe everyone, is keeping some secrets, so we don't have to show ours too soon either."

Chapter 49

J ACK LEFT HIS APARTMENT on Thursday morning after Susie had left for work. He usually stayed in Providence doing paperwork until Friday morning but he wanted to get the boat ready for Sally's visit this weekend. He had not seen Sally in almost 2 weeks and he wanted to put his best foot forward for this weekend. At least she had been answering her phone this week and their conversations had gotten more and more cordial as the week progressed. He first traveled to North Providence to stop at an Italian delicatessen to get some ingredients he would need for dinner on Friday and Saturday night. He had no plans to go sailing this weekend but if Sally showed a strong preference on Friday night he would arrange a day sail for Saturday. He picked up some sweet Italian sausage, Genoa salami, and capicola ham. He then stopped at a Portuguese bakery for some Portuguese rolls, Sally's favorite.

Jack drove south on Route 95, passing Jack Junior's house and turning off onto Rhode Island Route 4 So. He followed it down until it merged with Route 1 So. and then he got off the Point Judith exit onto Rhode Island 108 S. He stopped in the port of Galilee and bought two dozen cherry stone clams for steaming, a 1 1/2 pound lobster for Sally, and some sea scallops for himself. As he made these purchases, he realized it was going to require a lot of explaining to Sally. She had realized a long time ago that the more complex his culinary repasts became, the more sins he had to confess. He realized how personally stressful the last two weeks had been and how sadly misguided his attempts to mollify Sally's concerns had been.

He arrived at "The Stork" around 4 PM in the afternoon. He hadn't missed out on the chance to buy some chowder and clam cakes at George's while he was in Galilee. He would have them later for dinner. He spent the next two hours doing housekeeping on the boat. He changed the sheets on the bed, he thoroughly clean the galley, and checked that all the dinnerware and pots he would need for the next two days were serviceable. He went through the refrigerator making notes of things like eggs, butter, and milk that he would pick up at the supermarket on Friday morning. He put together a laundry basket that he would take to the Laundromat in the morning. Although he had never been tested, his domestic abilities were better than most bachelors and neither his Providence apartment nor his boat suggested the clutter of a single male. Still, for this weekend, he definitely wanted to put his best foot forward.

As Jack warmed up his chowder on the stove and the clam cakes in the oven, he put the album "Riding with the King" by BB King and Eric Clapton on the stereo. He found the latest copies of the Journal of the American Medical Association and the New England Journal of Medicine to review during and after dinner. In the last three years he had drifted away from reading the classic OB-GYN literature since he needed a broader medical base to work with at the Providence clinic. At this point he usually avoided the pure research articles and concentrated on those that had more clinical applicability. He got out one of the Portuguese rolls, cut in half and buttered both sides. He poured himself a glass of ice cold Coca-Cola from a glass bottle. Despite all the claims and hoopla, Jack had realized long ago that nothing else could match ice cold Coca-Cola from a bottle. He did not add the splash of fresh lime he usually added to canned Coke. He limited himself to three clam cakes but had two bowls of the red chowder he had gotten in Galilee. He would save his glass of single malt scotch for his nightcap.

Around 7:45 PM, 3 1/2 boring articles into the September issue of the New England Journal of Medicine, Jack's cell phone rang. He looked at the display and realized it was a number he did not recognize and that the caller ID had been disabled. Under normal circumstances he would ignore a call like this but before he could help himself he pressed the send button.

"I am looking for Dr. Jack Del Rio," said a distinctly familiar voice.

"This is he," said Jack, "who is this?"

"Dr. Del Rio, this is Detective Phil Hudson. I work in the Newport Police Department."

"I remember who you are," said Jack. "How can I help you?"

"I am sorry to call you this late at night," said Phil, "but this is an urgent request for you to come to the Newport precinct tomorrow."

"What is this about, and do I need an attorney?" asked Jack.

"This is about the Newport baby case, but I can't give you any more particulars than that. And yes, you should bring an attorney," said Phil.

"I'm a little confused," said Jack. "You know I have retained an attorney for my son, so are you telling me I need my own attorney?"

"Yes, I think you need your own attorney," said Phil.

"Well, you can imagine I may have difficulty getting an attorney to represent me at the interview by tomorrow," said Jack.

"My boss won't like it," said Phil, "but we will allow you to come in on Saturday morning or even Monday morning if you think that's absolutely necessary."

"This sounds very serious. Is this interview about me as a witness, or have I become a suspect?" asked Jack.

"Like I said before Dr., I am not at liberty to say."

"I will do my best to see you guys tomorrow," said Jack. "I don't think I want this hanging over my head all weekend and I am scheduled to work in the Providence free clinic on Monday morning."

"Thanks Dr.," said Phil. He left a cell phone number and a number in the precinct to call when Jack had made arrangements with his attorney.

Jack decided it was time to pour himself that nightcap. He looked up the number and called Jack Junior's attorney. He explained the current situation and Jason Platt immediately recommended a colleague from another defense firm in Providence. He told Jack he would make a few phone calls and that he thought the attorney would call Jack back that night. Jack gave him a cell phone number and hung up. Jack and Jason had both resisted the temptation to speculate on what this was about. Jack spent the next hour listlessly looking at several more articles but realized he had read none of them. He finally sat back and put pure BB King Blues on the stereo. If there was ever a time for blues music, this was it. Around 10:15PM, his phone rang.

Chapter 50

JACK AND HIS NEW attorney, Jillian Alves, sat in interview room 1, waiting for detectives Tony Fuentes and Phil Hudson to join them. They had spent most of the morning in emergency consultation discussing the case as far as Jack knew it so far. It was almost 1:30 in the afternoon, and unless this went very quickly, Jack knew he wasn't going to be able to prepare dinner for Sally the way he wanted to. He had had a sinking feeling that this was going to take a while and he and Jillian had worked on several scenarios on how this interview might go. As it would turn out, none of the scenarios were even close. Tony and Phil entered the room and introduce themselves to Jillian. Jack detected a small spark of recognition between Jillian and Tony suggesting to him that they knew each other.

Tony looked Jack in the eye, "I thought I had been lied to by the best but you've got them all beat!" He could see that both Dr. Del Rio and his attorney were completely taken aback. He sat quietly and waited for a response.

"Are you actually going to ask a question," asked Jack, "or am I just supposed to spill my life story to you like I am in a confessional?"

"Maybe we can start by you explaining to me how you came to be the biological father of Miriam's baby," said Tony.

"What do you mean I am the father of the baby?" said Jack indignantly, "I thought we had decided I was the grandfather of the baby. I suppose the next time we meet you are going to accuse me of being Miriam's father. Just what kind of clowns are you here and do you ever get any crimes solved?" Jack had blurted this out so quickly that Jillian had only at the last second rested her hand on his arm.

"In our first DNA analysis," said Phil, "we were told there was a 96% chance that Jack Junior was the father of the baby. We now have some new evidence that suggests even more strongly that you are the baby's father."

Jack sat quietly for a couple of minutes looking at Jillian. They had both noted that this was going to be a bad cop; bad cop interview and that both Tony and Phil were going to be ganging up on Jack.

"Where did you get Dr. Del Rio's DNA?" asked Ms. Alves,

Tony and Phil looked at each other. Phil finally replied, "Dr. Del Rio provided a DNA sample for a potential bone marrow transplant to one of his friend's sons."

"Is that even legal?" asked Jack.

"Did you have a subpoena to look at those samples?" asked Jillian.

Tony and Phil once again looked at each other. This was already starting to deteriorate. "We were provided this information by a reputable outside source," said Tony.

"Did they have a subpoena and who are they?" asked Julian.

"If it becomes necessary, we will provide those details. Right now I'd like the doctor to answer how it is possible for him to be this baby's father?" asked Tony.

"It is not possible for me to be this baby's father. I'm sure you have in your records from our last interview that I told you that I had never met Miriam before the night she came to the Providence Women and Infants hospital."

"Despite you saying that Doctor," said Phil, "we have direct DNA evidence that links you to this baby."

"I thought we had already established that my son was probably this baby's father," said Jack.

"Well we now have new evidence that suggests that you are more likely the baby's father than Jack Junior is," said Phil.

"I'm a doctor and I don't understand how that's possible," said Jack. "Besides, if I was involved with this case from the very beginning, why would I make those phone calls to the Newport and Providence Police Department's on the night she was admitted to the hospital?"

"We have asked that question ourselves," said Tony. "Maybe you were cleverly seeding information that might exonerate you if the details of this case ever came to light. There seems to be too many red herrings in this case. For instance, perhaps you could inform us about the adoption ring that was operating on your office around the time of this case."

At first Jack looked confused, but then his demeanor changed. He looked inquisitively at Jillian and she said, "Could my client and I have a minute alone please?" Tony and Phil quickly excused themselves, said they would go for coffee and asked if Jack or Jillian wanted any. Both shook their heads, no. Jack spent the next few minutes filling Jillian in on that episode in his office, as it was not something they had covered in the morning. When Tony and Phil returned, they continued with the questioning.

"You're referring to the illegal midwife who worked in my office," said Jack.

"Yes we are," said Tony.

"Well I take it you have done your homework, so you know

that she was found to not have a proper medical license. She was found to have falsified all her academic records, and she was evidently working with several attorneys in the Providence area to provide private adoption services. If you have the entire record, you know that all the doctors in my office were investigated and none of us knew anything about the adoption ring. I would like to point out in my defense that this person was a member of the staff when I joined the office, I had nothing to do with hiring her or verifying her credentials." Jack decided to stop talking because once again Julian placed her hand on his arm.

"Oh, that's what you say now doctor," said Tony, "but our source suggests that perhaps you and several of the other doctors were helping choose young women, helping them get pregnant or getting them pregnant yourselves, and then selling the babies to infertility patients in your practice."

Jack looked dumbfounded. "You're accusing me of getting Miriam pregnant as part of an adoption scheme?" Jack literally sneered as he made this comment and Jillian's hand tightened up on his forearm.

"Dr. Del Rio spent the morning filling me in on this case," said Ms. Alves. "So as I understand it, until today you thought Jack Junior had fathered this baby during a fling in the summer of '85. Jack Junior's even provided testimony that it might be possible for him to be the baby's father. He also testified he never saw her again after that first time. You then think he somehow helped with the delivery and disposal of this baby. You then alleged that he once again became involved with Miriam two years later and had something to do with her death. Now, this current line of questioning suggests that you think Dr. Del Rio may have conspired in starting this pregnancy, participating in the delivery, and also its disposal. Are you now also considering him as a suspect in Miriam's death?"

"I think we are getting ahead of ourselves here," said Tony. "But there are several other circumstances we want to investigate before we go down that path. Dr. Del Rio, it does seem like you enjoy the company of young women."

"Is there a question there?" asked Jack.

"We have information that suggests that you are currently living with a young woman who is a nursing student, despite the fact you have a long distant relationship with a college professor in Vermont," said Phil.

"She rents out the back bedroom of my apartment," said Dr. Del Rio, not mincing his words but realizing how terribly sordid that seemed under the circumstances. He glanced over at Jillian who was trying hard to suppress her surprise.

"We have reason to believe that this is not a casual relationship you have with this young woman," said Phil, and as the doctor started to interrupt him, he raised his hand and finished, "and we have information that she is not the first young woman to share your apartment with you."

"Even if what you say is true, I fail to see how that has anything to do with this case," said Jack.

"We are just trying to ascertain that if you currently have an eye for younger women, it would not be outlandish to think you had the same proclivities when you were younger," said Tony. "I can see how inflammatory it is to suggest that you impregnated these girls yourself, so perhaps you were simply providing sperm samples like that infertility doctor who was recently convicted of malpractice after it was determined that he had provided the sperm samples for 22 children and that he himself was their biological father."

"You think I had been a doctor for eight years and provided a sperm sample without knowing what it was going to be used for. That is the only scenario by which I could have done it without being part of the conspiracy. If I was a part of the conspiracy, it was a felony or at a minimum, medical malpractice," said Dr. Del Rio. "As a matter of fact, I knew exactly what would happen if I had given a sperm sample, because I had provided some samples when I was a freshman in college. It was an easy way to earn some beer money and I did it before I realize the full impact of what I had done."

"So, to be sure of your answers doctor; you have told us that you did not impregnate Miriam yourself and you never provided sperm samples 20 years ago that could have been used to impregnate her," said Tony.

"That is correct," said Dr. Del Rio, "I had nothing to do with Miriam's pregnancy except taking care of her on the night she was admitted several days after her delivery."

"I have one last topic to discuss with you Dr.," said Tony. "There was an incident on the bridge where Miriam died that involved a car matching the description of your wife's car. Jack Junior has already testified that he had no access to that vehicle in the months surrounding Miriam's death. Presumably you did have access to that vehicle?"

Jack looked defiantly into Tony's eyes and almost spit out," yes I did! And next I suppose you're going to ask me if I chased her up the bridge, cut her off, made her slam her car into the bridge rail, chased her 50 yards further down the bridge and threw her over into the river…" Jack stopped because this time Jillian literally kicked him under the table.

"Very astute of you, doctor," said Tony. "How did you know

her car banged into the guardrail and were you on the bridge the night Miriam died?"

A more subdued Jack finally answered, "No, I was not on that bridge on that night of January 25, 1988." Everyone stood up. They did not shake hands and each group filed out a different door. There didn't seem to be anything else to say.

Chapter 51

J**ILLIAN AVES DROVE** Jack Del Rio back to his mooring in Snug Harbor. She had never become comfortable watching her clients reconcile themselves to the fact that they were being accused of a crime. For the first 10 min. of their drive from Newport, Jack had said nothing.

"Are you okay?" she finally broke into his thoughts.

Jack looked at her, astonishment on his face. "I guess so, I cannot believe what just happened!"

She suggested to him that they spend a few hours going over the interview in detail. Jack told her that he felt that would be a good idea, but that he also had the arrival of Sally to deal with by early evening. "This episode with Jack Jr. caused a rift in my relationship with Sally. She thinks I have left her out of my struggles because I do not value her ideas. As a matter of fact, I was just trying to protect her from my distress. My second wife never understood my attempts to protect Jack Jr. I should know by now that Sally cares about me more than that." He described the extensive preparations he had made for dinner that evening, and he confessed that he was not sure he could complete that task.

"Well, we can postpone the meeting and you can concentrate on Sally's arrival," said Jillian.

"No, I think that would be even worse."

Jillian then asked Jack if he used cooking as a way to decompress and he nodded in the affirmative. "Well then, why don't we debrief while you cook?" He decided that that was a good idea and when they arrived at the boat she accompanied him on board. Jack poured himself a tumbler of single malt scotch and Jillian settled for a beer out of the refrigerator. As Jack started laying out the ingredients for dinner, Jillian removed her suit coat and jumped right into the preparations. He threw her an apron and they went about dinner preparations as they talked about the interview. She was careful to keep the cutting and chopping and knives part of preparation on her side of the counter while Jack did the sorting and measuring. As they settled into their cooking routine, Jack calmed down and started looking objectively at devastating interview he had just participated in.

"First of all, I am sorry I did not prepare you for the parts of the interview that obviously shocked you," said Jack. "I never expected that my office's midwife situation would come into play and I also never thought my living arrangements in Providence would be part of the conversation. I was chagrined to see how surprised you were when these topics came up, and I am eternally grateful for how professionally you handled yourself."

"Thank you for those remarks but I do not see how you could have predicted where they would go with this interview."

"Considering we only met earlier today, I am very grateful for your support. I never in my life dreamed that I would go to a confessional with a stranger in tow. I am going to profusely thank Jason for putting me in your capable hands. Tell me your take on the interview process today."

He listened carefully as she delineated her thoughts. She confessed to him that she had been surprised by the vigorousness of the attack against him by Detective Fuentes. She pointed out that the vigorousness of that attack had been meant to distract Jack from thinking properly and that it had worked to make him respond emotionally instead of thinking rationally. Jack accepted this constructive criticism and thanked her for reeling him in on the several occasions in which he had become irate. She then also pointed out to him that he had elaborated in too many places instead of strictly answering the question that was being asked. Jack shrugged his shoulders and acceded that he had flunked interview 101 today despite the many times he had gone over just that point with Jack Junior.

As they put the final touches on dinner, Jack heard Sally's Turbo pull into the parking lot. He and Jillian had not quite finished going over the interview, but Jack was much calmer than he had been when they had arrived at Snug Harbor. Jack raised a finger as he ran out onto the fantail of the boat and onto the gangplank to the boat. He ran across the parking lot and grabbed Sally in a bear hug. He buried his face in her shoulder and could hardly contain his sobs. Sally was appropriately stunned by this turn of events but remained quiet while Jack calmed down. She noticed Jillian come on deck putting on her suit coat and carrying her briefcase. When Jack broke his embrace he followed Sally's gaze to Jillian on the boat.

"Sally, this is Jillian Alves and I have retained her as my attorney because there has been a nasty turn in the Newport baby case. They think I am the baby's father! I contacted her through Jack Jr.'s attorney last evening and she helped represent me in an interview with the Newport police earlier in the day."

Jillian approached them in the parking lot and she and Sally shook hands. She explained that she was just leaving but Jack pleaded with her to stay for dinner to help him fully explain to

Sally what the days interview had been like since he was still not sure he could do it himself. Jillian replied that she could certainly stay and Sally acknowledged that she was all for that plan. Jack quickly explained that Jillian had help prepare dinner and certainly deserved to stay and enjoy some of it. Sally heartily agreed.

As they sat together on the fantail of the boat, Jack quickly outlined that the newest wrinkle in the case was that he had basically replaced Jack Junior as the lead suspect. Jack told Sally that the Newport police said they had DNA evidence that he was the baby's father, not Jack Junior, and that the police recognized that he would have had access to his wife's car at the time of Miriam's death. He also told Sally about the information the police had obtained about his living arrangements with Suzie in Providence and that he was being accused of being complicit in an adoption ring that had been uncovered in his office in the late '80s. The frankness of these revelations to Sally had once again made Jillian embarrassed. As Jack quickly looked back and forth between one of his oldest friends and his newest friend, he realized they might need a little time alone to digest these events. He excused himself to go down to the galley to set out a third place setting now that it been established that Jillian was going to stay. He quickly scurried away and out of sight.

Sally and Jillian looked at each other in amazement for several minutes. Sally began the conversation, "I know that you recognize that Jack and I have a unique relationship. Jack had two terrible marriages and I have reconciled myself to the fact that we would never marry. I also recognized early in our relationship that I would never be Jack's only paramour. Having conceded all that, it is inconceivable to me that Jack would have had anything to do with this young girl's baby's death or with her death. In his medical care of patients, I have never known anyone as ethical or dedicated as Jack. I guess the first thing I would like to know from you is how serious you think these allegations are?"

"I think they are very serious," said Jillian. "These detectives realized that they had made a major error in allowing Jack to sit in on their initial conversations with Jack Junior. That was a mistake they recognized as soon as they realized that Jack himself had become a suspect in this case. The very fact that he they have asked to interview Jack with an attorney present means they are dead serious in their suspicion of him as a major player in this case because otherwise they would've waited for this interview."

"I'm a little confused at how they could have DNA evidence that suggests that both Jack and Jack Junior could be this baby's father," said Sally.

"They are a little confused about that themselves, and Jack says that as a physician he doesn't quite understand how that could be," said Jillian. "There is an issue on how exactly they obtained the information about Jack's DNA but they will not reveal that source at this time. I think part of the reason that the detectives were so aggressive during this interview was that it does not help them to have a damning piece of evidence pointed at two different people. Their aggressiveness is actually a sign of ambivalence on their part. They were trying to make Jack become emotional so he would say something stupid. His return aggressiveness with his responses did make him look like he was trying to hide something. As a defense attorney, it is much easier to plant reasonable doubt in the mind of a jury when a key piece of evidence points to two different people. From the viewpoint of the detectives and a prosecuting attorney, they must reconcile that discrepancy for the jury. From the little I learned during the interview and the several hours I spent with Jack before and after the interview, I get the impression that them bringing up

Miriam's death is just a way to scare the suspects into conceding other points. Barring a direct confession or a picture of someone throwing Miriam off the bridge, I don't see how they can bring up any charges in Miriam's death, especially when her death has officially been ruled a suicide."

As Jack came up from the galley to announce that dinner was on the table, he could tell that Sally and Jillian had bonded well. As dinner got started, Sally effusively thanked Jillian for helping Jack out with such short notice. She then turned to Jack and said, "you were not involved in getting Miriam pregnant, were you Jack?"

"Whoa!" said Jillian. "You guys are obviously comfortable discussing anything but remember that I am Jack's defense attorney." She quickly pointed out they should not continue that conversation in her presence. Jillian assured them both that when she felt it was important for her to have that information, she would inquire about it from Jack directly. They finished the rest of the dinner with stories about their families, their work, and their plans for the rest of the weekend. Sally and Jillian were shocked to find out how much of their lives paralleled each others. Neither had ever married, they had multiple siblings and nieces and nephews, their families were the most important things in their lives, they both had a solid career they loved, each had had several important relationships with lovers but Jillian was currently unattached. Sally and Jillian understood that Jack's time was going to have to be split between them and they laid out a tentative plan for Saturday and Sunday.

After Jillian had left, Jack and Sally shared their concerns about the current situation. Sally also told Jack that she was 100% supportive of him and thanked him for including her as a confidante in this time of great turmoil. Jack told Sally that he had hopefully learned his lesson in the previous two weeks. Excluding Sally from his life was never appropriate. Jack thanked her for standing behind him and told her in no uncertain terms that he was not responsible for Miriam's pregnancy, the baby's death or Miriam's death.

Chapter 52

TONY, PHIL AND SHEILA sat in Tony's office. They each had their folder in front of them trying to rehash all the information they had acquired so far in the Newport baby case. Tony started off, "I knew from the beginning that this case was going to be a disaster. When I look at the interviews of Jack Junior and then Dr. Jack, I can see that we have a big problem. It seems like we have pretty damning evidence against both of them, the problem is the most damning piece of evidence points to both of them. I don't have to tell you both that the DA is not going to touch this case unless we resolve this. Miriam's death has been an interesting ploy to see what cages we could rattle, but you both know that solving that dilemma will be almost impossible. I think we all have to relook at the information we have and decide definitively if we are going to pursue Jack Junior or if we're going to pursue his father."

"You know boss," said Phil, "at one point you called Dr. Del Rio the worst liar you had ever met. During this last interview with him, I thought perhaps he was the worst teller of the truth I'd ever met. There were times during interview I was pretty sure that what he said was true, but the way he said it made me think he was lying."

"Now why do you think he would do that?" asked Tony.

"Maybe he's not sure of Jack Junior's role in this case, and he is trying to deflect our attention from Jack Junior to himself," said Phil.

"Wow," said Sheila, "that is a really risky move. I know that none of us doubt Dr. Del Rio's resolve, but do you really think he thinks he can pull this off?"

"Or maybe he thinks that we think he's not guilty because he's trying to take the blame, when he actually is the guilty one," said Phil.

"The three of us have lots of experience in interviewing people," said Tony, "but we may need a professional psychologist to get us through this dilemma. I think we need to continue to do the thing we do best, which is detective work. I think right now we have to go in specific directions and maybe even briefly revisit of some of the evidence. Phil, I think you should take the information we have from the Providence police to the Rhode Island State Police DNA lab. Talk to the expert you met there and see if he can unravel the mystery of how both the father and the son could have contributed 50% of the DNA to this baby. If he can tell you how, make sure he writes it down so that you and I and the DA and a judge and the jury would understand what he's talking about."

"I have been thinking about something," said Sheila. "It struck me as odd that both the Cohens and the Arnolds have adopted daughters from Korea. Except for Miriam, neither family had natural children. What if both families had infertility problems?"

"What you getting at Sheila?" asked Phil.

"I'm not sure what I'm getting at," said Sheila. "Mr. Cohen has been very defensive and has never supplied a DNA sample, what if Miriam is not his child?"

"I'm still not sure where that gets us, Sheila," said Tony.

"I'm not sure it gets us anywhere either," said Sheila. "I'm just thinking out loud. At this point in the case, we have a lot of bizarre information that somehow must fit together."

"It sure would be nice to have some DNA directly from Miriam," said Phil. "Anybody think we have a shot at finding her body to help us?"

"No!" said Tony and Sheila together.

"Oh well, the guy at the DNA lab seems to be a genius," said Phil. "Let's hope he' even smarter than I thought."

"One more thing Phil," said Tony, "before we put it completely to rest, I want you to revisit the evidence about Miriam's suicide and maybe even take a visit to the scene where it happened. Maybe something will occur to you that we haven't thought of yet."

"Ah boss," said Phil, "I can certainly revisit all the evidence but like, the bridge is gone!"

"Good point," said Tony. "I forgot that it is now the Jamestown – Verrazano Bridge and the old one was blown up and dismantled. And just a few months ago! Why did this not all come to light last year? Sheila, you and I are going to revisit the house on Thames Street. Let's bring all the pictures we have from the day they found the body. Let's see if we can walk our way through how the baby ended up in that spot."

"Sounds like a plan boss," said Sheila. "What about reinterviewing Mr. and Mrs. Cohen and Robert and Suzanne Arnold?"

"We will definitely have to do that again," said Tony. "But I would sure like to have some of these details pinned down. I think we have used the wild accusation card as much as we can. And now I would like to be able to ask questions that I actually know the answer to. Let's get a move on and close this case!"

Chapter 53

TONY AND SHEILA stood on the sidewalk waiting for the contractor to let them in to the house on Thames Street. After their last interview with the Arnolds, it'd been a little difficult, but Tony had gotten permission to revisit the house. There was no question that they would have been able to get a subpoena to do so, so Mr. Arnold finally relented and told them he would have the contractor let them in. When they entered the house they were amazed at how much progress has been made in renovating the inside. They took their flashlights and made their way down into the basement. It was now all cleaned up and actually had lights that illuminated the scene very well. They utilized a folding table to layout some of the pictures from the original crime scene. They walked over to the opening to the coal chute that had once again been carefully mortared closed. They carefully looked at the pictures that had been taken of the door slightly ajar and the remnants of the mortar that had been used to seal it years earlier.

"Is it just me," said Tony, "or does it look like this door was sealed in by a professional all those years ago just like it was sealed by a professional now?"

"I see what you mean," said Sheila. "If I remember correctly, the senior Arnold was a Mason before he became a real estate mogul. His son however went to college and got a business degree and has always been a businessman. That would seem to suggest that the younger Arnold might not have been responsible for putting the baby here, just as he suggested during his last interview."

"Show me the pictures of the baby inside the coal chute," said Tony. They both studied the pictures carefully. "Did we ever come up with an ID on the cellophane that was in the chute with the baby?"

"The suggestion is that it was the kind that was used to wrap around flowers at that time," said Sheila. "Remember that we did not come up with any detail on the blanket or the baptism outfit that the baby was wearing."

"Let's change tactics," said Tony. "Let's look at all these pictures and see if we can tell what's not there."

"I'm not sure what you mean boss," said Sheila.

"We're detectives. We're used to dealing with clues and of course, we focus on the clues that we can see. Sometimes it's what's not there that is important."

Sheila thought about that for a minute. "I can tell you this," said Sheila, "I don't see any violence in these pictures. This is not a formal burial scene, but it was well thought out. Sometimes we see this behavior as a sign of remorse but I don't see that in this picture."

"Exactly what I was thinking," said Tony. "All that likely means is that whoever buried this baby was not responsible for its death. But it sure does suggest that whoever buried this baby was very close to the person or persons responsible for its death."

"I think we're getting close," said Sheila. "But I think you were right before. We have to at least be sure of the cause of death of this baby before we can approach the Arnolds for another interview."

"I'm sure you're right," said Tony. "I had a thought also about whether we should shake down the adoption attorney who ended up showing up with the Arnolds. I just can't think of any scenario on how we could pull that off."

"After Phil's visit with the DNA lab, we will have to revisit the coroner. We will need to go with Phil because the coroner will not even answer his calls anymore. He promised to call Phil when he had more information but Phil does not expect to ever hear from him again."

"Good to know, I will have to take some of the pressure off Phil, if not for this case, at least for others."

As they were finishing up, Phil was parking his car on the Jamestown side of the Jamestown-Verrazano Bridge and he started the half mile walk up the pedestrian walkway. He looked south to where the old bridge had been. The western shore section had been preserved as a fishing pier when the main part of the bridge had been imploded. He looked as his notes and saw that Miriam had been traveling East on the night of her suicide. The car had been near the top of the bridge when it was found. The patrol had searched the entire length of both side of the bridge to see if they could determine where she had gone over. Even with the light traffic at 2-3 AM, it is unlikely she could have walked completely off the bridge without being seen.

Could she have been picked up by a following car and simply disappeared? He would look into the possibility she disappeared and was living somewhere else. After all, no one had been looking for her for many years!

Where was she going that night? Back to campus seemed obvious. Where was she coming from? Wow, too many possibilities! Dr. Jack was living in Providence and Jack Jr. was at the halfway house. This would have been an unusual route to home from those locations. Mr. and Mrs. Cohen were in Newport. Were the Arnolds already in Mystic? If she had visited them, she would be coming home this way. What about the Hail Marys? Would they have helped her escape? Why would they have met on the western end of the bridge?

Phil made notes to check on where everyone was supposed to be on that night. As he walked off the bridge, a gust of wind took his notes and scattered them off the side of the bridge. He felt a twinge in his stomach and they fluttered down to the water so far below. He had the same sinking feeling about the entire case. When he got back to his car, it took him twenty minutes to record his reflections on the bridge. Tony had been right; it had been a revealing visit. As usual though, no obvious destination was obvious …

Chapter 54

PHIL HUDSON STOOD in the office of Harold Sturgis at the Rhode Island State police DNA lab. He had sent over by fax the DNA matches provided to him by the Providence Police Department between Dr. Del Rio and the Newport baby. He was waiting for Harold to complete another case and come to speak to him. Phil looked over his notes trying to reconcile the myriad parts of this puzzle. Harold finally came in and sat at his desk and waved Phil into the chair.

"I understand that you have a dilemma in that another lab told you that Jack senior was this baby girl's father and I told you that Jack Junior was the father," said Harold.

"Did you say baby girl?" asked Phil. "I don't think we'd ever established that this was a baby girl."

"Oh, I'm sorry," said Harold. "I could've told you last time that it was a baby girl. I guess it never came up. Does that make a difference?"

"I guess not," said Phil. "And even the Dr. said he wasn't quite sure how these labs could point to both of them as being the father. Keep in mind that Jack Junior confessed that he might be the baby's father and Jack senior vehemently denies that he could be the baby's father."

"There are several scenarios by which that could happen," said Harold. "What exactly were you thinking?"

"Well, why don't we start with either Jack Junior being the father of the baby or Jack Senior being the father of the baby? How do you use DNA matches to determine maternity, paternity and sibling status?"

"If Jack Junior is the father of this baby, they would share approximately 50% of the same DNA markers. In that circumstance, Jack senior would be the baby's grandfather and the baby would have approximately 25% of the same DNA markers as Jack senior. If Jack senior is the father of the baby, they would share approximately 50% of the same markers. In that circumstance, Jack Junior and the baby would be half brother/half-sister and approximately 25% of their DNA markers would match each other, not 50%. In actuality, neither of those scenarios is supported by the fact that both Jack Senior and Jack Junior are 50% matches with this baby!" said Harold.

"Well shit" said Phil, "that's not much help at all."

"Not so fast," said Harold, "when two facts can't be reconciled, usually one of them is wrong. Let's look at both matches and see if we get the same conclusion that both could be the baby's father." Harold took the DNA marker samples from Jack senior and scanned it into his computer. He already had the DNA array of Jack Junior and the baby in his computer. He asked the computer to match Jack senior with Jack Junior, Jack senior with the baby, and Jack Junior with the baby. The computer quickly printed out the comparisons and Harold stood looking at them for a few minutes. "Well I'll be damned," he said.

"If that means we're all going to hell, I agree completely with your assessment," said Phil. "How exactly do they match up?"

"Jack Junior and the baby match 48% of their markers. Jack

senior in the baby match 52% of their markers. Jack Junior and Jack senior match 52% of their markers," said Harold.

"Help me with the tech speak," said Phil. "Does that mean that Jack senior is more likely to be the baby's father."

"Not at all," said Harold. "Both of these percentages are well within the parameters of a parent-child match."

"But I thought you said that couldn't be," said Phil.

"Curious," said Harold. "Curious and not compatible with either of our original scenarios."

"So we're nowhere," said Phil.

"Not so fast," said Harold. "Let's compare how much DNA match there is between Jack Junior and this baby that would come from Jack Senior if he is the grandfather." He punched a few more buttons on his computer and promptly got another readout. He stared at the readout for a long time. Phil began thinking that Harold was just as confused as everyone else in this case when Harold suddenly said, "I've got it!"

"Please tell me what you got in some kind of a language that I can understand and will be able to translate to my boss," said Phil

"This is one of the most amazing matches I've ever seen," said Harold. "This baby does have about a 50% match with Jack Junior and 50% match with Jack Senior but some of the DNA matches with Jack Senior are not found in Jack Junior's sample!"

"English, English please, what does that mean?" asked Phil.

"It most likely means that this baby's mother, Miriam if I remember correctly, is also an offspring of Jack Senior!" said Harold.

"Shit," said Phil, "the Dr. made fun of the possibility that our next phone call would tell him he was Miriam's father and that would prove that we were clowns that could never close any case.

Are you sure these conclusions mean he was Miriam's biological father?"

"The only way that this baby could have markers from Jack Senior that did not come from Jack Junior is if they came to the baby from Miriam. That means that Miriam is Jack Senior's biological daughter," said Harold.

"Oh my God," said Phil, "Dr. Del Rio said he gave some sperm samples to an infertility doctor in Providence when he was a freshman at Brown University. That would be about 40 years ago; about the age that Miriam would be now if she were still alive. My partner, Sheila, was speculating that the Cohens might have had infertility problems. If Mrs. Cohen conceived Miriam by artificial insemination, wouldn't that mean that Dr. Del Rio could be the biological father?"

"By golly," said Harold, "I think you have solved this dilemma."

"Yeah," said Phil dejectedly. "So Jack Senior is Miriam's father, the baby's grandfather and Jack Junior is the baby's father. One dilemma solved but still no closer to finding out how this baby died. I'm not sure my boss is going to be happy."

Chapter 55

DR. JACK DEL RIO and his attorney Jillian Alves once again sat in interview room one of the Newport precinct. They had been summoned here rather abruptly by Phil Hudson and he had cryptically told them over the phone that new facts had come to light. Jack had driven from Snug Harbor to Newport and Jillian had come down from her office in Providence. They were surprised to see that this time the entire detective team came in and sat across the desk from them.

"Dr. Del Rio," said Tony, "there have been new developments in the DNA assessment of this case and we thought we would present this information to you to get your take on what it means."

"Does that mean I have gone from being a suspect to being a peripheral player in this case?" asked Jack.

"Not exactly Dr.," said Phil. "I spent an interesting afternoon with Dr. Harold Sturgis at the Rhode Island State Police DNA lab and after looking very carefully at all the DNA evidence we have, he tells me unequivocally that you are Miriam's biological father."

Jack and Jillian were stunned, speechless, and they looked at each other trying to digest this information. "So the joke I made about you telling me that I was Miriam's father in our last interview has now come true," said Jack.

"I cannot say that I understand it all," said Tony. "But Phil here says that Dr. Sturgis is virtually certain that you were Miriam's father and you are this babies biological grandfather but with contributions from both Jack Junior and Miriam. Maybe you can explain to us how that could be. You did say that you were a sperm donor many years ago when you are at Brown University."

"But that can't be," said Jack. "I know I was young, I was looking for beer money, but I did recognize that I was probably going to live in this community for the rest of my life. I got solid assurances from the infertility doctor that my sperm samples would not be used in Rhode Island, nearby Massachusetts, or nearby Connecticut. It was explained to me that many offices would collaborate on these collections and trade them back and forth so that no one community would have multiple offspring from the same donor."

"After doing some research into private adoptions," said Sheila, "I also looked into sperm donation. As you probably know there are now regional sperm banks that are well controlled and donors are tested for things like HIV that didn't exist forty years ago. They collect information like race, skin color' hair color and eye color so that recipients can try to match the family characteristics that they desire. They could also limit the number of offspring anyone donor might have in any one location. Back then, none of these factors were well controlled for. It is also my understanding that most Jewish families requested that a Jewish donor be used for their artificial insemination. Perhaps this infertility doctor felt that your donation from a Catholic in Providence made it reasonable to be used in Newport with a Jewish couple. Back then it would theoretically fulfill the requirements that you would not have too many offspring that traveled in the same social circles."

Well," said Jack, "I guess that didn't quite work out. Certainly the time frames are consistent that if my sperm was used in the fashion that you describe, then I could be Miriam's biological father. If you don't mind, I would like to spend a couple of private minutes with my attorney discussing the ramifications of this information."

"We can certainly do that Dr.," said Tony. "One last thought for you both; it seems that you and Jack Junior are the alibis for each other at the time of this baby's birth. It is reasonable to consider that we will be able to verify your alibis. That leaves us with the unpleasant thought that Miriam may have been responsible for this baby's death. See if you can help us with that."

When Jack and Jillian were alone, one look into Jack's eyes made Gillian recognize he was about ready to cry. She gently held his hand and said, "Jack, what exactly did you want to discuss with me about this interview?"

Jack stared at his hand in Jillian's hands. "I have no thoughts about this interview at this time," said Jack. "I just needed a little time to digest this information. I keep thinking back to that night. She was actually my biological daughter. I called the police on her! Did I treat her well? I've always treated everyone like I would want a member of my family to be treated. I am not sure I did that for her, and she was my daughter!"

Jillian sat quietly for a few minutes holding Jack's hand. She didn't say anything because she actually didn't know what to say. Finally, she gently addressed Jack once again, "Jack, it seems like they're no longer aggressively pursuing the scenario in which you or Jack Junior participated in this baby's birth, death and its subsequent burial. We have already talked about the theory that Miriam's death was actually a murder instead of a suicide was too far-fetched for them to be able to prove. Is there anything about this new information or about the circumstances of Miriam's hospitalization that might help them decide if she was or was not an active participant in this baby's death?"

Jack thought about that for a few minutes and actually became reenergized. He would have to deal with his own feelings about Miriam and he would have to have some discussions with Jack Junior about what this revelation meant to them both. But for the moment, diverting his attention to trying to help out the Cohens would be a welcome diversion. Jillian stuck her head out of the interview room and told a nearby sergeant that they were ready for the detectives to come back in.

"My attorney and I have discussed this situation," said Jack. "I know that even if you tell me I'm not officially a suspect anymore, if some other information becomes available to you, you might put me right back on that list. In any case, I have decided to discuss this case with you regardless of whether I am a suspect or not. In that spirit, can you tell me if you have decided what the cause of the baby's death was?"

Tony, Phil and Sheila looked at each other. It was Tony that spoke first, "we still do not know why this baby died. The baby was not stillborn, and the coroner puts the time of death around 3 to 4 days post delivery because it looks like the umbilical cord had just fallen off. It would certainly seem that that timeframe would put Miriam in the hospital with you in Providence. If she had simply abandoned the baby somewhere, it is not clear to me that the baby would've lasted 3 to 4 days before it died. And then, she would have had to recover the baby and bury it in its location on Thames Street. We have no evidence to suggest that Miriam had any access to that house."

"Somewhere along the line, you had floated a theory that she had given the baby up for adoption," said Dr. Del Rio. "Have you been able to figure out who she might have given the baby up for adoption to?"

Once again, Tony, Phil and Sheila looked at each other. Tony had a resigned look on his face and shrugged his shoulders at Sheila who started to speak, "we have some information that suggests she may have given the baby up for adoption to a couple whose family owned the house on Thames Street. Evidently the wife in this family used to babysit Miriam when Miriam was a child."

"So do you think that Miriam knew about the baby's death?" asked Jillian.

"Actually, from some of the comments we received and because she knew the family the baby allegedly went to, we think she would have known about the baby's death," said Phil.

"I know the other part of this case that you have been trying to solve is Miriam's death. If Miriam knew that this baby did not survive, that certainly could have been a factor in her suicide," said Dr. Del Rio.

"That's an excellent point Dr.," said Tony. "Her mom originally denied that she was depressed, but some of her friends at Solve Regina did say they thought she was depressed."

Everyone was quiet for several minutes when suddenly Dr. Del Rio became quite animated. "If I am the grandfather of this baby through Miriam as well as through Jack Junior, then Miriam and Jack Junior are half brother/half-sister. They did not know that of course, but many religions forbid relatives that closely related from having children because of unusual diseases in the offspring. The official medical term of close relatives bearing children is called consanguinity. There are many very obscure congenital conditions that are potentially lethal when consanguinity is a factor in the production of the offspring. There is a genetic inheritance pattern called autosomal recessive that is where both sides of the family have the condition. One that you might readily recognize is cystic fibrosis because it is the most common one in the United States. I think it is imperative to relay this information to the coroner so they will expand the possible diagnoses that might explain the baby's death." Jack looked around the room, not sure that anyone had actually followed what he had just said. "If what I am thinking is confirmed, I will refer you to a genetic counselor who is adept at teaching nonmedical people about these conditions and she will explain it to you."

"So if I understand you correctly Dr.," said Phil, "I need to tell the coroner that consanguinity may be a complicating factor in this baby's birth. Could you spell that for me?" Jack did.

Chapter 56

PHIL AND TONY STOOD in the coroner's office together.
Tony had reassured Phil that he knew that Phil could handle
this by himself, but he was coming along for authoritative support
since the coroner seemed to be avoiding Phil's phone calls. The
coroner was a bit surprised to see them both together. Jonathan
Schemerhorn had been the Newport County coroner for almost
25 years. He had identified almost every kind of criminal activity
that man had ever known to visit upon another human. But he had
to admit that in this case, after almost a month, he was no closer
to the cause of death for this baby as he had been shortly after the
original autopsy. He looked warily at Phil and Tony and thought
he must be in trouble to have them both arrive unannounced in
his office.

"How can I help you detectives?" asked Jonathan.

"Actually," said Phil, "we have come here to help you."

"That's a joke, right?" asked Jonathan. "What might you
possibly tell me that could help me decide the cause of death for
this baby?"

"I'm sorry to see you have such a lowly opinion of the work
that we detectives do," said Phil. "We have it on good authority

that we have brought you a clue that will help you solve this dilemma."

"What might that be?" asked Jonathan, his voice and facial expression dripping irony.

"One word," said Phil for the first time realizing how much he was enjoying this situation. "Consanguinity, that is c o n s a n g u i n i t y!"

"I know what consanguinity is," said Jonathan, "and I know how to spell it, too. What makes you think that played a role in this child's death?"

"Due to some fine detective work," said Phil, "we have discovered that the parents of this child were half brother/half-sister who shared the same father. Since this baby had the same grandfather from both its maternal and paternal sides, we were told it might share some very rare autosomal recessive genes. That is a u t o..."

"Okay, don't be a smartass," said Jonathan. "That actually is very helpful." He pulled out the notes from his autopsy and spent several minutes looking at the pages. He completely ignored the presence of Phil and Tony as they exchanged furtive glances at each other, hardly hiding their amusement in this situation.

"The reason this information is so important," said Jonathan being much more serious now, "is that a lot of these autosomal recessive diseases, as they were described to you, can be potentially lethal soon after birth. If that is the case, it may well be that no one murdered this child! I have a couple of ideas that I will have to investigate a little further. One of the first ones that come to mind is that this baby had a hole in the back part of its skull. I have been unable to come up with a tool or instrument that might have caused that hole traumatically. There is a congenital malformation in which a part of the skull does not form properly and part of the brain sticks out of the skull cavity itself. That is called an encepholocoele and it is caused by a congenital abnormality. One of the rare autosomal recessive conditions that cause this defect is called Meckel-Gruber syndrome. It was probably a relatively small defect and might not have been noticed if the baby did not get immediate, professional pediatric care. Another part of the syndrome includes multi-cystic/dysplastic kidneys that would have resulted in renal failure of the fetus shortly after birth. Virtually none of this babies internal organs survived their long time in that coal chute, but I did note only small cystic remnants were present where the baby's kidneys should have been. Now that I know what to look for, I can probably run a chemical analysis on the baby's remaining skin and see if there are unusually high urea levels present. That would pretty much solidify kidney failure as cause of death."

"I am impressed," said Phil. "I know you and I have not gotten off on the right foot with this case, but I mean that in all sincerity. I am impressed that we could come here with one word and that within a few minutes you have probably discovered the cause of death."

"I second that," said Tony. "It would be fantastic news if you could confirm these details for us. How long do you think it will take for you to run the tests that you need? One last thing, if this mother had had prenatal care with ultrasounds or if this baby had been examined immediately after birth, would this baby still have died? "

"If I am correct, nothing could have been done to save this baby. I should have the tests finished by late this afternoon," said Jonathan. "And I am sorry, too. We definitely got off on the wrong foot and this case has bedeviled me for the last 4 weeks. If my tests confirm my current theory, I will call you later today and you should have a completed report from me in two or three days."

"Thanks," they both said together. For the first time in almost a month, Tony had a smile on his face.

Chapter 57

DR. DEL RIO and detectives Antonio Fuentes, Philip Hudson, and Sheila Goldstein sat in the driveway of the Cohen's residence. After the coroner had made the confirmation they were expecting, they had invited Dr. Del Rio and his attorney in for a last conference at the precinct. Although there were some loose ends to tie up, Tony had told Jack that he had promised the Cohens that he would visit them when they had discovered what had happened to the baby. Now that it look like murder was off the table for the demise of the infant, they felt Mrs. Cohen might be more forthcoming about Miriam's involvement after the baby's birth. Dr. Del Rio convinced them that he might be useful when they presented Mrs. Cohen the information about the baby's death. "Jillian and I have discussed the implication of having to identify myself as the sperm donor for Miriam's conception," said Jack. "I know it is risky but I will do it if it becomes necessary."

Sheila had vigorously lobbied to let him come along to be available if needed to clarify details. They had all decided that he would not proceed into the Cohen's house until the detective team had discuss his presence with Mr. and Mrs. Cohen to see if they would be comfortable with that idea.

The three detectives rang the doorbell and it was once again answered by Amanda Cohen. She led them into the dining room where her parents sat waiting quietly for them. Sheila made quick introductions all around and they all sat quietly for a few seconds.

"Well I suppose we should get this over with," said Mr. Cohen. He was a little less defiant than he had been in their previous encounters. He had obviously resigned himself to the fact that this was going to happen whether he liked it or not.

"We now have evidence that Miriam's baby died of a congenital abnormality that was incompatible with life. In other words, no matter what Miriam had done this baby would have died. The timeline we have put together strongly suggests that this baby probably died while Miriam was in the hospital being attended to for her post delivery bleeding. So, although we know that Miriam was not responsible for this baby's death, we still have not figured out who was caring for the baby at the time of its death and how it ended up in the house on Thames Street. We were hoping you could help us with that," said Sheila.

"Although my wife initially lied to you about knowing about Miriam's pregnancy, she has told you unequivocally that she was not with Miriam at the time of delivery and she does not know who took care of the baby. I cannot see how dragging all of this up now is helping my wife, she has struggled for over 20 years with this family disaster," said Mr. Cohen.

"We are not here to open old wounds," said Tony. "At our last interview I promised your wife that if we could determine the circumstances of the baby's death we would come here and tell her. That's what this visit is about. Despite what Sheila has described, from our viewpoint there are a few details remaining to be discovered. Just as your wife has probably felt guilty all these years, we think there may be another family involved in this baby's death who has also felt terribly guilty for the last 20 years."

"I can see your point," said Mr. Cohen. "I just don't see how this continued digging helps my family."

"I would like to help," said Mrs. Cohen. Before her husband could object any further, she waved him off. "Yes, I did know about Miriam's pregnancy, but I was not present at the time of the baby's birth. I know that she had made arrangements for a private adoption, but the first time I learned about the delivery was when her friends called me from Providence to say that she was having problems with bleeding. Despite many discussions with her she would never violate the trust of the couple who took the baby. I did not know until you told me that the baby had died shortly after birth. That might explain why she seemed so depressed. Can you give me some more details about exactly what was wrong with the baby and why it died?"

"I'm not sure we understand the disease well enough to explain it to you better than we already have," said Sheila. "We have an expert that we brought with us that might be better for its explanation but first I think you might want to have Amanda leave the room because the explanation starts with Miriam's birth."

"I think I can see where you're going with this," said Mr. Cohen. "Despite my behavior with our other interviews, I want you to know that there are no secrets here. Like with most adopted children, Amanda realized a long time ago that my wife and I had issues with infertility. While I have never stated it in public before, Miriam was not my biological child. I suspect you surmised that when I would not participate with allowing any DNA samples. If this medical expert can help us bring closure to this chapter of our lives. I would welcome it."

"I think this encounter will be much more of a surprise than any of you could ever have expected," said Phil. "The expert that we have brought was not only Miriam's doctor in Providence, he was not only the father of Miriam's baby's father, he was also the sperm donor who was probably responsible for Miriam's conception!"

There was stunned silence from everybody at the table. "What are you talking about? Say that again!" exclaimed Mr. Cohen.

"Well I would like to hear from him," said Mrs. Cohen without any hesitation. "But I am certainly sensitive to my husband's wishes. If he does not think this is a good idea, I will defer to his wishes."

They all looked at Mr. Cohen who finally said, "I am also okay with this. I have often felt inadequate at mollifying my wife's grief over Miriam's death. Although Miriam was my daughter and I loved her dearly, I never felt her loss as acutely as my wife did. I know it's not true, but I sometimes felt like my wife lost her biological daughter and I did not. She has never actually accused me of that, but I have felt guilty anyway."

"Let me go speak to the doctor," said Phil, "and see if he's ready to come in." Phil made his way out to the car. He filled in the information he had already given to the Cohens to see if Jack was sure he wanted to reveal his identity to them. Jack simply got out of the car and followed him up to the house.

Jack walked into the dining room and introduced himself to everyone at the table, shaking hands as he went around. He sat at the head of the table and began to speak immediately, "I am sorry for the loss of your daughter and granddaughter."

"The baby was a girl? No one has ever told us that," said Amanda. She looked around the room and all the detectives hung their heads.

"You can't be my daughter's biological father," said Mrs. Cohen. "The infertility doctor assured me that the sperm donor was Jewish."

"I share your shock and surprise," said Dr. Del Rio. "I was assured that my sample would not be used anywhere in Rhode Island. So I guess that deception is just another part of the story that we share."

"Perhaps it would be best to let Dr. Del Rio tell his story uninterrupted," said Tony. "I assure you there will be time for questions when he finishes." He looked over at Jack who nodded his assent at the suggestion and restarted his narrative.

"When I was a freshman at Brown University, I was a sperm donor and my sperm was evidently used to help you conceive Miriam. 19 years later I took care of a very scared young lady in Providence, Rhode Island who had evidently just given birth and was suffering from bleeding and infection. She vehemently denied the pregnancy and although I reported her to the authorities, nothing ever came of those phone calls until last month. By a strange turn of events, it turns out that my son was responsible for Miriam's pregnancy. Because this baby shared genetics from both its mother's and father's side, it inherited a rare condition called Meckel-Gruber syndrome and it died three or four days after birth. No one would have been able to change the outcome for this baby but I suspect that Miriam felt guilty about it and that probably led to her depression. I delivered babies for 25 years and I can tell you that your daughter very likely felt responsible for this baby's death because that is how moms are programmed. We now have information that suggests that no matter what she did, the outcome would've been the same. I am not sure that even if we had this information while she was alive, she would have embraced it, but we will never know that would have happened if the police had investigated these events 20 years ago instead of now." He looked around the room but none of the detectives would return his gaze.

"Oh my God," said Mrs. Cohen."I knew that she seemed depressed but I never knew that she probably knew the outcome of the baby. Maybe if I had known that, I could've helped her more." She started to sob.

"I have a question for you related to her depression," said Jack." Her girlfriends told the police that she seemed to be getting better in the weeks before her death. Do you know if she had started on medication?"

"Why yes, she did," said Mrs. Cohen, "but she had only been on it for a week or two."

"The reason I ask," said Jack, "is that we now have evidence that sometimes in the first few weeks of taking an antidepressant, when the patient starts feeling better but remembers how badly they felt during their depression, is the most dangerous time. Sudden suicidal thoughts can lead to their death. Now, no one would've known that information when it happened to your daughter, but perhaps you can go a little easier on yourself in terms of feeling responsible for her loss."

"I will have to think about that," said Mrs. Cohen. "But thank you for explaining some of the events from 20 years ago that had been unfathomable before now."

"And I would like to thank you also," said Mr. Cohen. "Despite my reservations about this, I think these conversations have potentially been very beneficial for my wife."

"There is one last thing before we go," said Sheila. "I hope we have convinced you that if you know who Miriam gave the baby up to, we can close the rest of this mystery and perhaps help another grieving family."

"I was never sure," said Mrs. Cohen, "but I was always suspicious that she had given the baby to Robert and Suzanne Arnold. I knew Suzanne as a Brady, and only recently learned her married name. That's why when you asked me in an earlier interview, I did not make the connection with the Arnolds. In that case of course, Miriam would have known that the baby died because the Arnolds only ever had one child, their current adopted daughter."

"Thank you for that information," said Tony. "I know that it was not easy for you to divulge that information and I want you to know it only confirms very strong circumstantial evidence we had on that connection."

As they all got up to leave, Jack held the hand of both Mr. and Mrs. Cohen at the same time. "I am sorry for your loss," said Jack. "I only knew your daughter for three days. Since I found out that I was her biological father, I have wondered every waking minute if I treated her like I would want my daughter to have been treated. I wish I could have known her longer, it is obvious that she was loved by all of you, her family." On their way out, Sheila noticed that Dr. Del Rio had a tearful expression on his face. She had to turn away so she from him so she would not join him.

Chapter 58

TONY, PHIL AND SHEILA sat in the break room of the Newport precinct. They had once again asked Dr. Del Rio to participate in the final interview with the Arnolds. The Arnolds had refused to entertain a thought that they would welcome the detectives into their home in Connecticut, so they had made arrangements to come to the precinct with their attorney. When they were all present, they went to the conference room instead of an interview room so that they could all be accommodated at the table. Tony introduced Dr. Del Rio as the physician who had treated Miriam at the hospital for complications after delivery.

"I want you to know we now have information from several sources that suggest that Miriam gave her baby up to you for a private adoption," said Phil.

"I don't see why we have to go down this street again," said Mr. Arnold. "I think we have made it very clear in previous interviews that we were approached by Miriam about adopting her baby but we had declined that offer." He was once again as defiant as they'd ever seen him in previous interviews.

"Dr. Del Rio accompanied us with our final interview with the Cohens, Miriam's parents. If you would indulge us for a minute, I am going to have him outlined the medical information we now have available on this baby's death," said Tony.

"I see no reason why I should allow you to subject my clients to this story. Since they have disavowed any knowledge of this baby's birth or death, I see no reason why they should sit here and listen," said their attorney, Howard Baines. There was a moment of awkwardness before anyone spoke.

"Believe it or not," said Dr. Del Rio, "I not only took care of Miriam when she was hospitalized in Providence, I was actually her biological father, and I was the father of the young boy who got her pregnant." If this outburst was meant to shock and confuse the Arnolds and their attorney, it had its intended effect.

"That's fascinating," said Mr. Arnold, still as cold as ice. "But unless there are some charges to be filed here today, I think we have heard enough of this conversation." As he started to stand up his wife Suzanne put her hand on his arm and had him sit back down.

"I think I'd like to hear a little more of this story," said Suzanne. "I knew Miriam as a child and if this helps me understand her death better, I am willing to listen."

"Perhaps you could give my clients and me a few moments to discuss this," said Mr. Baines. As Tony and the others got up to leave, Suzanne called them all back into their chairs.

"I have made up my mind to stay and listen!" said Suzanne. She then turned to Robert and Howard and said, "You don't have to stay if you don't want to. I am going to stay and listen and I will find another way back home if needed."

"I guess we're staying," said Mr. Arnold. He exchanged a furtive glance with his attorney who shook his head in the affirmative.

"As I was saying," said Dr. Del Rio, "because I was the grandfather of this child from both its mothers and fathers side, we believe it died of an autosomal recessive genetic condition called Meckel-Gruber syndrome. The typical abnormalities found on a child with this syndrome include a cranial defect which was found at the time of autopsy and abnormal cystic kidneys that fail shortly after birth. This child would have looked perfectly normal immediately after birth, but over the next two or three days it would have become less and less responsive because it was developing renal failure. This would not have resulted in a painful death; the child simply would've died while asleep, similar to what we normally expect for a SIDS death."

At this point Suzanne Arnold started to cry. Her husband put his arms around her shoulders, he was also visibly shaken. "It's all exactly as you have described it," said Suzanne.

"Suzanne, are you sure we want to go down this path?" asked Robert.

"I think you should listen to your husband," said Mr. Baines.

"I don't see what good it does anymore," said Suzanne. Turning her attention to Dr. Del Rio and the detectives, she resumed her narrative, "I am tired of hiding and telling lies and being remorseful about this baby's death. I have even been concerned that my activity was responsible for Miriam's suicide. I hope you all understand that we were just young scared kids. After five years of marriage my husband and I had not been able to conceive any children. My cousin Mary, a friend of Miriam's, had suggested to her that we might be interested in a private adoption of her baby. We embrace the concept willingly, but when Miriam declined to allow us to get her any medical care, we initially declined her offer. As the end of her pregnancy drew closer, she finally relented and let us take her to see a nurse midwife in Connecticut. She was quite late in the pregnancy, no ultrasounds had ever been done, but we did get the rudimentary blood work necessary for pregnancy care. When she went into labor, the nurse midwife did her delivery at her office. Everything went well. Several hours after birth Miriam left to go back to her dorm room and we stayed with the baby. It was overwhelming. I have subsequently looked at psychological studies that suggest the nine months of a pregnancy is useful to prepare a couple to take care of their newborn. Many adoptive parents go through shock when they quite suddenly have the child overtake their lives. They have no child and then they have a child to take care of 24 hours a day. They are not ready for that and they become overwhelmed. We were overwhelmed. After the adoption papers had been completed, we were planning to bring the baby to a pediatrician. In the meantime, we had no documentation that the baby was ours. We had told no one about the baby, but on the last day of its life when it seemed so sleepy I finally spoke to Robert's parents about what we had done. Robert's mom and dad came over to see the baby. They were delighted that they finally had a grandchild. My mother-in-law and I went over some details of how to take care the baby for the next few days and all seemed well. The next morning when Robert and I went into the baby's room we found her dead in the crib. We panicked. Calling the police seemed out of the question as did calling 911; the baby was clearly gone. We once again called Robert's parents and they came over. After several hours of crying, we discussed what our next step should be. Mr. Arnold Senior suggested we release the baby to him and he would take care of it."

"It all happened as my wife has described," said Mr. Arnold. "Since no papers had been filed about the baby, we did not see how we could go to the authorities. My father was heartbroken at the baby's death, and when he suggested he could take care of things, we hesitantly decided to let him do so. I never found out what he did with the body, so I can assure you I was as shocked as everyone else when the baby was found in the house on Thames Street."

"You can imagine how scared we were. No paperwork had been filed to complete the adoption and we wanted to protect Miriam's involvement in the case. We didn't see how calling the authorities would help," said Suzanne Arnold.

"Can you tell us exactly how you were involved in this case?" asked Tony to Mr. Baines. "Since you are an officer of the court, didn't you think you need to report this baby's death?"

"I think you misunderstood my wife," said Robert Arnold. "We originally had Mr. Baines start working on private adoption papers but when the baby died, we reported to him that it had been a stillborn and asked him not to file even the preliminary paperwork he had already completed."

The detectives looked at each other with some skepticism. They all looked at Mr. Baines who decided that he would not participate in this discussion.

"I have another question," said Suzanne Arnold. "If we had called a doctor and this baby had started on dialysis, would it have lived?"

"No," said Dr. Del Rio, "nothing you or your husband or Miriam or Mr. Baines could have done would've changed this outcome. Unfortunately because of its genetic condition, this baby was going to die shortly after birth."

"Is anyone in trouble here?" asked Mr. Arnold.

"I spoke to the district attorney before you all came in here," said Detective Fuentes. "Since there seems to have been no foul play in the baby's death and since Miriam's death has already been officially ruled a suicide, there does not seem to be any charges to be brought in this case. Would you agree Mr. Baines?"

"Yes, I would agree," said Mr. Baines as enthusiastically as he could.

"I would like to thank you all for giving us this information," said Suzanne. "I especially want to thank you, Dr. Del Rio, because the circumstances of this case and your family's involvement in it must have made it very difficult to digest when all the pieces came together. I have spent many years wondering if that night was ever going to catch up to us. In my worst dreams, there were always repercussions to be paid by me and my husband and Miriam. Of course, Miriam's outcome was tragic. I only wish she could be here now to understand the inevitability of that weekend's outcome. Do you think there is anything I can do for the Cohens?"

"I think when you're ready, you might contact them. If they agree, you can all get together to commiserate over the outcome for this baby, their daughter and your friend, Miriam" said Dr. Del Rio. "I think they would like that."

"I do have one last question for you," said Phil. "Did Miriam visit you the night of her death?"

Robert and Suzanne looked stunned and the answer was obvious. "They do not have to answer that!" said Mr. Baines.

"It's alright, I think the answer is obvious," said Suzanne. "Miriam and I met every three or four months to console each other. That night, she met our newly adopted daughter and even though it was not a surprise to her, she was much more emotional than I expected. She stayed quite late, playing with the baby. I though they bonded well and thought her future visits might be even easier for her. If I had known what was going to happen, I never would have let her leave."

"No one would have predicted her actions after that encounter. Please do not blame yourself!" exclaimed Dr. Del Rio. Suzanne hugged him fiercely before they left.

As they each headed out from the conference room, everyone shook everyone else's hand. As Sheila shook hands with Mr. Baines, she thanked him once again for being kind enough to speak to her about private adoption services.

Chapter 59

JACK FOLLOWED TONY to his office before he left. Tony shot a curious look at Jack and nodded his head to Phil and Sheila to join them.

"You could have saved us a little time when we interviewed you doctor," said Phil. "Don't you think it would have been important for you to tell us that you could not be responsible for Miriam's baby since you had had a vasectomy four years earlier?"

"How did you find out about that?" asked Dr. Jack. "Did you illegally look at my medical records?"

"Actually, we found out when we talked to Suzie," said Tony.

"You guys talk to Suzie?" asked Jack.

"Yes we did," said Sheila. "Actually, we spoke to a few other renters of your back room."

"Well I'm embarrassed," said Jack. "But yes, shortly after I married my second wife, it was clear that neither one of us wanted any more children. So I had a vasectomy and she had a tubal ligation."

The three detectives looked at each other curiously. "We don't want to know anymore about why you both had sterilizations," they all said in unison. "We are curious why you didn't tell us."

"I think you know the answer to that," said Jack. "You all seemed bound and determined to pin a murder or murders on my son. While I have every confidence in my son at this time, I was not sure my son could not have done what you were accusing him of back then. I guess I wanted to deflect attention away from him by giving you an easy shot at me."

"You're a good dad," said Tony. "I think. I am glad we allowed you to accompany us to the final interviews with the Arnolds and Cohens. Over the years, I have been satisfied when I have completed a case by identifying the perpetrators. A real downer for me is how bad I have felt about other accused individuals that we left hanging. Most of the suspects had done other illegal things but these seemed like they could be completely innocent. You helped provide those families closure. It was invaluable. Thank you."

"I just wonder why you never even considered my second wife a suspect; she had motive since she was suspicious when the police accused my office of causing the pregnancies of some of the adoptions. She could have found out about Miriam and she obviously had access to her car! She would have done anything to discredit me or my son after we got divorced"

The three detectives just looked at each other. "We did look into that," Phil lied.

A few hours later, Jack sat quietly on the fantail of his boat waiting for Sally to arrive. He was nursing a glass of his favorite single malt scotch, and he had a half bottle of Sally's favorite White Zinfandel sitting on ice. He had a pot of homemade New England clam chowder simmering on the stove, light on the cream. There were a dozen cherry stone clams that he had just steamed open. There were two fresh Haddock fillets on the broiler sprinkled with a little bit of butter and paprika. There were two dozen frozen steak fries cooking in the oven. There was a bottle of malt vinegar, some drawn butter, some tartar sauce and salt and pepper ready to season each entrée as needed. Sally pulled into the parking lot just as the timer for the fries went off. The haddock needed two or 3 min. more to be finished so they dove into the chowder and steamers. Sally could tell that Jack was in a much better mood than he had been for the previous month and she suspected there had been some good turn of events in the Newport baby case.

As they finished dinner, she started on her second glass of wine and Jack opened a beer from the refrigerator. He smiled as he fleshed out the final two or three days of the investigation. He told her the shocking revelation that a sperm donation by him 40 years earlier had resulted in the conception of Miriam. He spoke in soft tones of how he felt like he had missed an opportunity to change her final outcome.

"I think if I had convinced the police to pursue the missing baby angle 20 years ago, we might have discovered the truth and maybe Miriam would have never gotten depressed enough to kill herself!" He spoke at length of the cruel genetic outcome that had resulted in the death of his biological granddaughter, a second lost generation he had never even met. He spoke about his concerns that he had not treated Miriam well enough when he took care of her in the hospital. He spoke of how moved he had been when he learned about the loss of her life and his connection to the start of it. He marveled about how strong her parents must be to have known her for 20 years and then lost her. He had been thinking about them a lot.

Sally held his head in her lap. "You can't know what would have happened," she whispered in his ear. "You can beat yourself up forever thinking about the possibilities. I think you should concentrate on how well you did with Jack Junior!"

They spent Saturday quietly contemplating how Jack was going to break the news to Jack Junior that Miriam had been his biologic half-sister. There was no way he could have known that, but Jack wasn't sure how the news would go over with Jack Junior. They decided that they would get together on Sunday and Sally would take Donna and the children to Roger Williams Park so that Jack and Jack Junior could have a few hours alone to discuss the situation. After the last meeting with the Arnolds, Jack had called Jack Junior to tell him that his involvement in the criminal case was over. Jack Junior was interested in more details but Jack had simply told him that they were for another time.

On Sunday they all met at the Providence Place mall for lunch, spent an hour and a half shopping, and then Sally invited Donna and the children to accompany her to Roger Williams Park. They all planned to meet back at Jack Junior's house for dinner and Jack and Jack Junior proceeded to the house in Cranston. In the next two hours with a lot of "I can't believe it" from Jack Junior, Jack recounted the entire story to Jack Junior. After it all sank in, Jack Junior was in a quandary about what he was going to tell his wife.

"I am not sure how to counsel you on that topic," said Jack. "I assure you that none of the story will get to her from me or the police. Only you can decide exactly what to tell her or to just leave that part of the story out." Jack suggested he delay any confessions to Donna until he had resolved his own feelings about the matter. He also told Jack Jr. to reassure his wife that Mary and David were in no danger from the disease that had resulted in the baby's death.

When Sally, Donna, Mary, and David returned to the house, they all had a quiet dinner, and as usual discussed the lives of Mary and David. Jack Junior seemed pretty uptight at first but he slowly made his way into the conversation and by the time Jack and Sally were ready to leave, Jack felt that Jack Junior would be okay.

Since it was late when dinner finished, Jack asked Sally if she wanted to stay at his apartment in Providence and drive to Vermont the next morning. Since she had no classes until noontime, this would certainly be doable for her. They left Jack Junior's house with that plan in mind, but several minutes after they had both made their way onto Route 95, Sally called Jack on his cell phone and told her she had changed her mind and that she was going to proceed home to Vermont. He begged her to be careful and she promised she would and pointed out that she had had no drinks with dinner. They made plans for the next weekend and Sally thanked Jack for including her in resolving his own feelings on the highly confusing and unexpected outcome.

Jack parked his car in the garage and walked up to his apartment. As he entered the apartment, a naked Suzie jumped into his arms, wrapped her thighs around his waist and kissed him full on the lips.

"You mean to tell me that two of the last four weekends you have been unable to find a suitable partner?" asked Jack.

"On the contrary," said Susie, "not only did I find someone, she's in the master bedroom setting up the massage table! She says she's never done a gynecologist before!"

Jack had a fleeting vision of Sally walking into the apartment with him. He shuddered, looked into Suzie's expectant expression and Jack groaned…

The author was born and raised in Rhode Island, a second generation American of Portuguese descent. He attended Providence College before moving to upstate New York to attend medical school. He practiced Ob-Gyn for 35 years. He has taught college and medical school classes. He continues to live in upstate New York with his wife and visits South County in Rhode Island for several weeks every summer. He has over 100 relatives in the Rhode Island area. His non-medical interests include skiing, golf, music, motorcycling, travel and, of course, writing.

If this book is not available at your local book store, it can be purchased online at www.TBMBooks.com or www.amazon.com

Please visit the author on Facebook at Steven Noble, author.